[redacted] TECHNICAL INSTITUTE

[redacted]ORTH CAROLINA
STATE [redacted] OF EDUCATION
DEPT. OF COMM[redacted] COLLEGES
LIBRARIES

Y0-CUL-949

WITHDRAWN

HOLDING TECHNICAL INSTITUTE LIBRARY
ROUTE 10, BOX 200
RALEIGH, NORTH CAROLINA 27603

ELSEWHERE, ELSEWHEN, ELSEHOW

Collected stories by

MIRIAM ALLEN deFORD

Walker & Company New York

813.01
D315e
c.1

Copyright © 1971 by Miriam Allen deFord

All rights reserved. No part of this book may be reproduced or transmitted in any form or by any means, electronic or mechanical, including photocopying, recording, or by any information storage and retrieval system, without permission in writing from the Publisher.

All the characters and events portrayed in these stories are fictitious.

First published in the United States of America in 1971 by the Walker Publishing Company, Inc.

Published simultaneously in Canada by Fitchenry & Whiteside, Limited, Toronto.

Library of Congress Catalog Card Number: 77-147792.

Design by Paul Pascal.

Printed in the United States of America.

ISBN: 0-8027-5540-2.

Old Man Morgan's Grave appeared in the October, 1952 issue of Fantasy and Science Fiction. Copyright © 1952 by Mercury Press, Inc.

Mrs. Hinck appeared in the March, 1954 issue of Fantasy and Science Fiction. Copyright © 1954 by Fantasy House, Inc.

Gone to the Dogs appeared in the March, 1954 issue of Beyond (as *Henry Martindale, Great Dane*). Copyright © 1954 by Galaxy Publishing Corp.

The Margenes appeared in the February, 1956 issue of If. Copyright © 1956 Quinn Publishing Co.

Martie and I appeared in the February, 1956 issue of Fantasy and Science Fiction. Copyright © 1956 by Fantasy House, Inc.

The Old Woman appeared in the October, 1957 issue of Fantastic Universe. Copyright © 1957 by King-Size Publications, Inc.

The Apotheosis of Ki appeared in the December,1956 issue of Fantasy and Science Fiction. Copyright © 1956 by Fantasy House, Inc.

Freak Show appeared in the February, 1958 issue of Fantastic Universe. Copyright © 1958 by King-Size Publications, Inc.

The Eel appeared in the April, 1958 issue of Galaxy. Copyright © 1958 by Galaxy Publishing Corp.

First Dig appeared in the May, 1959 issue of Fantasy and Science Fiction. Copyright © 1959 by Fantasy House, Inc.

Prison Break appeared in the July, 1959 issue of Fantastic Universe. Copyright © 1959 by King-Size Publications, Inc.

Not Snow Nor Rain appeared in the November, 1959 issue of If. Copyright © 1959 by Galaxy Publishing Corp.

The Monster appeared in the March, 1960 issue of Fantasy and Science Fiction. Copyright © 1960 by Mercury Press, Inc.

The Cage appeared in the June, 1961 issue of Fantasy and Science Fiction. Copyright © 1961 by Mercury Press, Inc.

The Voyage of the "Deborah Pratt" appeared in the April, 1963 issue of Fantasy and Science Fiction. Copyright © 1963 by Mercury Press, Inc.

The 1980 President appeared in the October, 1964 issue of Galaxy. Copyright © 1964 by Galaxy Publishing Corp.

The Peak Lords appeared in the February, 1966 issue of If. Copyright © 1966 by Galaxy Publishing Corp.

The Colony appeared in the May, 1966 issue of Fantasy and Science Fiction. Copyright © 1966 by Mercury Press, Inc.

The Crib Circuit appeared in the November, 1969 issue of Fantasy and Science Fiction. Copyright © 1966 by Mercury Press, Inc.

The Old Bunch and Dusty Stiggins appeared in the October, 1970 issue of Fantasy and Science Fiction. Copyright © 1970 by Mercury Press, Inc.

For

HANS STEFAN SANTESSON

In grateful appreciation

CONTENTS

A WORD IN ADVANCE

Some of these stories are science fiction, some are fantasy. Many readers and some writers have only a vague understanding of the difference between these two aspects of what has been called "speculative fiction."

Phrased rather too simply, science fiction deals with improbable possibilities, fantasy with plausible impossibilities. This is not a completely accurate distinction—for one thing, time travel, which is considered to be a legitimate subject for science fiction, is never likely to become a reality—but it gives a rough working definition. As examples from this book, never, under any conditions, will a human being become a dog: that is fantasy. On the other hand, though it is doubtful whether we who have to breathe polluted air will eventually become a surface-dwelling proletariat ruled by aristocrats who can afford castles in the pure air of the mountains, it *could* happen (unless we are all wiped out first): that is science fiction.

But even the wildest fantasy must have some coherent form. However outré its basic concept, one thing must follow another as sequence or consequence. To one like myself who believes that the chief psychological difference between humans and other animals is the ability to reason, much of the amorphous and completely irrational contemporary fiction appears to be of primary interest only to the psychiatrist.

In other words, once given the premise (possible if improbable when it is science fiction, impossible but not sequentially improbable when it is fantasy), the rest must follow, "as the night the day." We do not abandon reason; we build on it, sometimes we play with it, and always we defer to it.

Slowly both science fiction and fantasy, like mystery and suspense, are being drawn into the fictional mainstream. That means that the days of the heavily technical so-called "story," with cardboard figures manipulated to illustrate a plot, are over forever. Increasingly, science fiction characters are becoming *people,* depicted in the round, with the psychological traits and social background we all have. (Even an extraterrestrial may be so depicted, and is.) Take a recent novel by Harry Harrison, THE DALETH EFFECT (Putnam, 1970); it is concerned with a means of space travel which may or may not be scientifically valid, but it also deals with national rivalries, war and peace, and world government, and it deals with them in terms of recognizable feeling, thinking, and reacting individuals.

There *is* no "Daleh effect" (as yet, anyway), but logically there could be one, and Harrison has shown us what the result would be if there were.

There is an increasing number of such books nowadays, and they are transforming the old kind of science fiction into a part of mainstream fiction purposely oriented to the needs and problems of our post-atomic era.

As for fantasy, that has been with us since our caveman ancestors sat around their fire and recounted their dreams and spun tales of gods and stars and animal relatives and the ghosts of the dead. It will be with us, refined and sophisticated, while the demand persists for emotional food to satisfy our hunger for the marvelous and surprising—which means as long as mankind itself continues to exist.

In the early days of science fiction, sex was strictly taboo. If women appeared in the stories at all, they were there merely to be captured by bug-eyed monsters, in the pulps, or as passive, quiescent wives or sweethearts even less individualized than the men. Now, in these permissive days and in the light of the new feminism, all that has been changed. Often women are active protagonists, and questions of sex-relations and matrimonial and parental systems are allowable subjects for writers in this genre as in others.

I should therefore explain why none of the stories in this book treats of sexual problems. It is because a previous collection of my science fiction, all of it centering on sex, marriage, and reproduction on other planets or in the future, has already been published, as XENOGENESIS (Ballantine, 1969). Even so, the women who appear in these non-sex-centered stories are all "movers and shakers" in their own right.

Of these stories, the earliest written go back as far as 1952. (In fact, a different version of the fantasy situation in *Old Man Morgan's Grave* first appeared nearly forty years ago.) The latest of the stories were published very recently. I do not think, however, that you will find much difference of viewpoint between the earliest and the latest, because all of them are consciously founded on the tenets I have outlined above. They are representative specimens of my writing in both science fiction and fantasy, and I hope you will like at least some of them.

— MIRIAM ALLEN DEFORD

ELSEWHERE, ELSEWHEN, ELSEHOW

OLD MAN MORGAN'S GRAVE

Old man Morgan was never of any importance in our town while he was alive. All the excitement came after he had died.

He was quiet, friendly, fastidiously clean, and shiningly honest, and he was a good cobbler. Often I have watched those gnarled, skillful fingers at work, and thought how much of a man's personality is in his hands. He came here right after World War I, old even then for a newly discharged soldier, and long before he was gray people were calling him Old Man Morgan. He must have been over 70 when he died in a heart attack last March.

He was the only Negro in the town.

I rented him the little shop with living quarters behind it in that building I own on Second Street, and he lived there alone, in two scrubbed and polished rooms. He often remarked that he had no living relatives. Like so many cobblers, he had a philosophical and metaphysical turn of mind—maybe it's something in the long hours they spend doing mechanical work, which gives them leisure for meditation—and though I'm sure his formal education hadn't gone beyond grammar school, Miss Vestris at the library told me once that there wasn't a serious, solid book on her shelves he hadn't read. She was always sending to the State Library for things he wanted that she didn't have.

A few of us, through the years, got into the habit of dropping in of an evening to the bare, finically immaculate little sitting-room behind the shop, for long sessions of talk with Morgan—old Dr.

Sprague; John Thorpe, the frail young pastor of our Community Church; sometimes Miss Vestris herself; and I. He was an aging Negro cobbler, and we were all white and of the so-called professional class; but we had two things in common—we were interested in abstract discussion, with a special flair for the psychic and extrasensory, and we were unattached, lonely people. I guess we were the nearest to friends he had, though everyone liked him and wished him well.

Everybody, that is to say, except Floretta Bewley—though that didn't come out till after Morgan was dead. Not that it was a surprise. Floretta was a Hatcher, and this is Hatcherstown. On that basis, she is the town aristocrat. On the same count, I ought to be an aristocrat too, for my maternal grandmother's maiden name was Hatcher; but then I have other things to occupy my mind, and Mrs. Bewley hasn't. She has every thread of the town's life tied around her fat fingers, and with Sam Bewley's money to hand out, there aren't many people who don't cave in the minute she raises her squawking voice. I'm one of the few—in my opinion, my distant cousin Floretta is a bigot and a menace. Probably she never laid eyes on Old Man Morgan—she doesn't have to have her handmade shoes repaired—but what happened certainly came as no unexpected shock to any of us—though even I hadn't thought her capable of quite such depths of nastiness.

It started when Thorpe called me up about half-past 7 on a Wednesday evening. Morgan had died Monday night. His heart had been acting up for several years, and he'd made Dr. Sprague tell him the truth. He speculated a lot, despite our protests, on what would happen after what was coming to him soon. I recall his saying: "I hope some of me stays a long time here in Hatcherstown. I've been contented here."

The *Herald-Despatch* comes out on Wednesdays, and it carried a brief paragraph—something to the effect that Alpheus Morgan, colored, the old-time shoe-repair man on Second Street, had succumbed to a heart attack, and that the funeral would be at 10 o'clock Thursday morning at the Community Church, with interment in Mount Olivet.

"Hartley," Thorpe said on the phone, "can you come over to my place right away?" He sounded upset. "It's about the Morgan funeral," he added.

We don't lock doors much in Hatcherstown. I walked right in

and upstairs to Thorpe's study. He was sitting at his desk; his mouth was fixed in a tight line and that little tic he gets in his right temple when he's excited was flickering like mad. Perched on the edge of his most comfortable chair, with her stout legs planted stiffly before her, her face red, and her wattles quivering, was Floretta Bewley. When I said "Good evening" she just glared.

"Dr. Sprague will be here in a minute," Thorpe told me. His voice was strained.

Sprague came right on my heels, and he had Annie Vestris with him.

"Miss Vestris was in my office when you called," he said, "and when she heard it was something about Old Man Morgan she insisted on coming along."

Mrs. Bewley fixed her with an oystery eye and made a noise between a grunt and a sniff. Annie's a nervous, fidgety sort of person generally, but she stared defiantly back. It took courage; Floretta is on the library board—as what isn't she on, that you don't have to be elected to?

"Well," she snorted, "let's get this over with. I still don't see the necessity of calling in all these—these persons. I've told you a simple fact, Mr. Thorpe, and there's not a thing any of you can do about it."

I raised an eyebrow at Thorpe. We'd all found ourselves chairs by now.

He said very quietly: "Mrs. Bewley says we can't have the Morgan funeral tomorrow."

"I said no such thing and you know it," she retorted. "You're the minister here—for the present at least—and nobody can stop you from officiating at any services you choose to hold in the church—though perhaps the board of trustees will have something to say about that at their next meeting." She was on that board, too, of course, and by far the largest contributor to the church. "But you can *not* bury this man in Mount Olivet Cemetery."

"Why not?" I inquired. "Morgan bought a plot nearly ten years ago. As his executor, I have the bill of sale in my possession this minute."

She turned the barrage full on me.

"You're a fool, Wayne Hartley," she informed me. "Allow

me, as a director of the cemetery corporation—"

"I'm one too—remember?" I interrupted.

"I know that perfectly well. And I suppose you thought you put something over on me when you sold that plot, didn't you? Just because I'm too busy to give proper attention to every one of my interests, or to follow every little detail, you and whoever else was in on it deliberately violated the articles of incorporation.

"I suppose you merely overlooked the fact that burials in Mount Olivet are limited to members of the Caucasian race?"

"Now, just a minute, Floretta," I said. I could feel my throat tightening up. "If that clause is in the articles—and I suppose you must have looked it up—it dates back to a day when conditions were very different from what they are now. It's obsolete and obstructive, and it was never meant to be acted on to bar a good citizen and a good man like Morgan. Why, you know yourself that as long as this town has existed everybody from Hatcherstown has been buried in that cemetery. It's the only one we have."

"They have not!" she crowed triumphantly. "Within just the past few years, what about that Emmet Sheehan? What about that man Cohen who owned the Bon Ton Store?"

"That's a completely different thing. Naturally Emmet Sheehan and Isaac Cohen were laid away in cemeteries of their own faith. But Alpheus Morgan was a member of the Community Church, just as much as you are; and except for one or two newcomers who had family plots elsewhere, every communicant of this church has been laid to rest in Mount Olivet in our lifetime."

I clamped my jaw to keep from reminding her of some of the dirty, sneaking ways she had harassed Sheehan and Cohen, too, to make their lives miserable. Floretta Bewley's prejudices aren't specialized.

Her face grew redder still, till I thought she was going to burst.

"You might as well save your breath," she snapped. "If you think for one minute that any of your specious lawyer-talk is going to keep me from preventing this—this insult... Why, do you realize that the plot you idiots sold illegally to this man is in the very next section to my own family plot—that it's not a hundred feet from the monument to the Founder himself?"

I had to hide a grin. A while ago I thought of writing a history of the town for the State Historical Society, and I did a bit of research, back in Pennsylvania where he came from, on Matthew Hatcher. I wonder how Floretta Bewley would take the revelation that when old Matthew came out here with his young "bride" and founded our town, he'd left a wife and four children behind him? But he was my great-great-great-grandfather too, so I've decided to let him rest in posthumous rectitude.

"That isn't a Christian attitude, Mrs. Bewley," Thorpe said mildly.

"And what's more, it's insane," Dr. Sprague put in. "What are you trying to do, Mrs. Bewley—make Hatcherstown the scene of a national scandal? Have you forgotten the reaction when that cemetery in Sioux City refused to bury the Indian soldier who was killed in Korea? You do anything to interfere with that funeral tomorrow, and by night the news services will have hold of it, and there will be headlines in every paper in the United States—and worse headlines still in countries where a case like that would be considered a perfect godsend.

"How would you like to see our cemetery surrounded by pickets waving propaganda banners—and perhaps other people picketing the pickets? How would you like to see Hatcherstown the arena of a disgraceful public squabble between the anti-democratic forces of the left and of the right?"

"Piffle. The news services can't get the story unless somebody from the *Herald-Despatch* sends it in—and don't forget I hold the majority stock in the *Herald-Despatch*.

"I didn't come here to argue; I came to tell you that I'm going to prevent that burial. If you think I'm going to sit back and see my dear husband's grave right next to that of a dirty old—"

"He wasn't dirty!" Annie Vestris's lips were trembling but she looked Floretta Bewley right in the face. "He kept himself and his place as clean and neat as a pin. I never knew a fussier housekeeper, or a man as tidy about his own person, as Mr. Morgan was. If you could have seen him carefully straightening a curtain, or picking up the least bit of lint from the rug—"

"*Mr*. Morgan!" Floretta pinned the librarian down with a cold stare. "I don't know, Miss Vestris, that our town library ought to be under the charge of a woman who acknowledges such a close personal acquaintance with the household arrangements of—"

"That's enough, Mrs. Bewley." The minister rose to his feet, and even Floretta Bewley shut up at the look on his face. She stood too, and gathered her mink coat about her.

"Very well," she announced. "I've given you fair warning. I have no more to say. Hold your funeral service tomorrow morning if you wish, Mr. Thorpe, but when it's over you will have to reconsign the remains to the undertaker's establishment, until *Mr.* Morgan's executor here can arrange for burial in a Negro cemetery. At the next meeting of the cemetery directors, I'll see that the purchase price of the lot is refunded and sent to Wayne Hartley to add to his client's estate.

"As for me, the first thing in the morning I shall go up to Chantonville, and I shall have no difficulty in securing a restraining order from Judge Ogden. In fact, I called him up before I came here tonight, and he agrees with me entirely."

We knew she could do it, all right. Judge Ogden is as narrow-minded as he is senile—and hand-in-glove with Floretta Bewley.

"I shall be at the gate of Mount Olivet tomorrow with an officer of the law, and if you dare to attempt to bring this person's remains through that gate, I shall see that the injunction is served. If you want to avoid unpleasant publicity for Hatcherstown, Dr. Sprague, then don't put yourself in a position where all of you will have to appear at a court hearing and maybe find yourselves imprisoned for contempt of court."

She swept to the door of the study.

"Mrs. Bewley," Thorpe pleaded, "won't you at least think this over? Can't anything at all make you reconsider?"

"The only thing that could ever make me reconsider, Mr. Thorpe," she responded icily, "would be a miracle—and I am afraid that is something which you are not equipped to provide."

She slammed the door behind her.

Three pairs of baffled, expectant eyes turned to me in appeal. After all, I'm a lawyer.

"There are just two things I have to get off my chest—things I wouldn't waste my breath telling Floretta Bewley," I said. "Then, if you're willing to take the risk, I think there is something we can do. She can't harm me much, or Dr. Sprague either, but she can ruin you, Miss Vestris, or you, Mr. Thorpe. There are plenty of people who will back her up."

"If I can't be free to follow the principles in which I believe," said the minister, "then I shall take my chances on finding another church."

"I feel the same way," agreed Annie Vestris stoutly. Poor Annie, 30 years in the library on a starvation salary!

"Well, one thing I want to say is that six months ago I drew up Morgan's will. He had a pretty good trade, and he lived very simply and thriftily. Everything he left, after the expenses are paid, is going to found a college scholarship for deserving boys and girls from Hatcherstown."

"That Mrs. Bewley!" murmured Miss Vestris vindictively.

"She'd probably consider that only one more evidence of Morgan's presumption.

"And the other thing is the reason Alpheus Morgan has no surviving relatives to speak for him now. He had a wife once, and two children, and a mother. They all died the same day, long ago, in a race riot in the little town where he was born. He wasn't there—he was in the army of his country. . . .

"Now, legally, a man does not own his own body. But in the absence of near relatives, his wishes as to its disposal prevail.

"Morgan loved Hatcherstown. When I drew up his will, he insisted that I incorporate in it his deep desire to be buried in the only place where, as he put it to me, he had been treated like a human being."

"I know that's true," Dr. Sprague put in. "Just before he lapsed into unconsciousness he said to me, 'Doctor, I don't know how far my spirit's going to wander, but I'm glad my old bones will rest forever near the only friends I ever had.' "

"Exactly. And I propose that we see to it that his last wish is carried out. For another point of law is that once a body is buried it cannot be disinterred, even by the authorities, except for the most urgent and cogent reasons. My contention is that the clause in the incorporation papers on which Mrs. Bewley relies is a mere dead letter, which it is not necessary to observe, and that in any event once Morgan had been given a receipt for the plot he had a legal right to burial there. Mrs. Bewley's injunction will never stand up on appeal to a higher court. But we can't wait till she finds that out."

"But if we disobey the injunction, won't we be breaking the law?" asked Thorpe.

"There is no injunction for us to disobey until she gets hold of Judge Ogden tomorrow," I replied.

"You mean—?"

"Just who do you think will be coming to Morgan's funeral?"

"Why—you three here—and perhaps some of his neighbors—and the people who never miss anybody's funeral. Why?"

"In other words, the only ones with a personal interest in the old man are here now in this room. I propose that we adjourn to the church and hold the services this evening—and that then we proceed to bury Alpheus Morgan in his plot in Mount Olivet."

"Hold on a second, Hartley," Dr. Sprague objected. "Hornbuckle's got something to say about that, hasn't he? Morgan's body is in Hornbuckle's funeral parlor right now, and he's got all the arrangements made for tomorrow."

"Have you forgotten Jim Hornbuckle is my sister's husband?" Annie Vestris interposed. "Jim's all right. He hates Mrs. Bewley, anyway. He's never forgiven her for calling in that big city mortician when her husband passed away. You call him up, Mr. Thorpe, and explain everything to him. He'll be glad to co-operate."

"There's another thing, though." That was the doctor again. "How are we going to get into the cemetery? It's locked up now, and Ed Frater's off duty."

"We wouldn't want to involve him anyway," I answered. "You forget I'm a director, just as much as Mrs. Bewley is. I have a key.

"The grave's dug already. Ed Frater did it this afternoon; I checked with him. If Hornbuckle will accompany us, we four men can carry the casket off the hearse and put it in the grave ourselves, and cover it over enough to constitute a legitimate burial. Later on, Frater can smooth and sod the plot; the tombstone won't be ready for setting for a few days in any case. The moon will be up by 11, and one of us can hold a flashlight for the others if we need more light."

"I'll do that," said Miss Vestris. "No—don't shake your heads. I'm going with you. We're all Mr. Morgan's friends, and we must all stand together."

"Shall I call Mr. Hornbuckle?" Thorpe inquired. "I can make preparations to hold the services any time after he delivers the remains."

"It's 8:30 now." I looked at my watch. "I'll have to go home and get the key to the cemetery gate. Suppose we tell Hornbuckle the funeral will be at half-past nine."

"Will you take me with you?" asked Miss Vestris. "If you can stop off by my place, my lilac bush is full of blossoms, spring has been so early, and I could pick a big bunch and bring them back."

Dr. Sprague cleared his throat.

"In the lack of anyone better," he said, "I can play the organ well enough for a hymn or two, if you'll let me into the church first to practice for a while."

We came back loaded with Miss Vestris's lilacs. But it had clouded up, and it smelled like snow.

It was a strange funeral, but there was more genuine feeling to it than to many more elaborate ones I have attended. And it was a strange, silent procession out to Mount Olivet, with Hornbuckle driving his own hearse, and the rest of us following in the doctor's car. I was right—it had started to snow, after the premature spring, and by the time we reached Mount Olivet it was snowing heavily and staying on the ground.

We found the plot without any difficulty—it was practically in the shadow of the Hatcher monument, as Mrs. Bewley had observed, and Sam Bewley's ornate tombstone stared at us right across the path. Ed Frater had done his job as thoroughly as always. We couldn't get into his toolshed, so we had no rope and pulley and no grass mat, but we men, even though Hornbuckle was the only one of us who could be described as really husky, managed with a good deal of puffing and creaking to get the casket in place. Since the moon was hidden, Miss Vestris held the flashlight for us.

Then we discovered we had no shovels to fill the grave. By this time the snow was really piling up. There was nothing else to do; we all, even Miss Vestris, set to work on the pile of loose earth with our hands. Finally we got most of it transferred from the graveside into the hole, though Frater would certainly be horrified when he beheld that lumpy, loose, irregular mound. I made a mental note to call him at his home before he left in the morning. Already the snow was covering the big pile of earth, and our footprints were plain in the trampled space around it.

"And now what, Hartley?" inquired Dr. Sprague as our tired, dirty crew hobbled back to the cars.

"Mrs. Bewley won't be able to get to Chantonville and get hold of Judge Ogden much before 9. She expects the funeral to be at 10 o'clock at the church, as the paper announced. I doubt if she'll bother to check it; she expects us to defy her, and she's sure to be here at the cemetery gate with her injunction by 10:30 at the latest. I propose to be here before she is, and to face her down with the accomplished fact. What will happen next is anybody's guess.

"It won't be necessary for anyone else to come too, but if any of you should want to, it's all right as far as I am concerned."

Thorpe and Sprague said right away that they would come. Miss Vestris couldn't make it, because she was due at the library. It was lucky she wasn't there, in view of what happened.

I got Frater on the phone early in the morning, told him the funeral had been "postponed," and to do nothing about the Morgan grave till I got in touch with him again. He was puzzled, but he's used to taking orders from the directors, and he said he was glad to have the time to clear the paths of snow.

Just in case Mrs. Bewley should take it into her head to turn up early, I drove to the cemetery right after breakfast, and parked my car near the gate. It was still snowing a little—just a few lazy flakes fluttering down. The heavy fall had stopped by the time we reached home the night before. Sprague and Thorpe arrived in Sprague's car soon after me. We all had the right hunch. It wasn't ten minutes after they got there that we saw Mrs. Bewley's big limousine rolling up the drive, and when it stopped and the chauffeur opened the door, Frank Voorhies, one of the deputy marshals, got out right after her.

Floretta approached full sail, with the expression of a soap opera mother forbidding the banns.

"There's no use your holding the fort here, Wayne Hartley," she blared. "Judge Ogden has issued the injunction on my petition. Morgan is not to be buried in this cemetery—or you will be held in contempt of court."

Then she realized that Thorpe was among those present. She looked at him blankly.

"Do I understand that you have come to your senses among you and called this funeral off?" she demanded.

Before any of us could open our mouths, there was a yell from inside the gate. I turned and beheld Ed Frater racing down the path, white to the gills.

"Mr. Hartley! Mr. Hartley!" he gasped. "I just went down to take a look at that grave before I started work on the other side, and—and—" His breath gave out.

I saw suspicion leap into Floretta Bewley's bulging eyes.

"Have you been up to any underhanded monkey-business, Wayne Hartley?" she pounced on me. "If you've tried to put anything over on me—here, you, whatever your name is, tell me instantly what is wrong!"

Frater goggled at her, still unable to speak. I pushed the gate open and as if that were a signal Frater turned and began running toward the Hatcher monument. We all hurried after him in an untidy huddle. In a minute we were shouldering one another at Old Man Morgan's graveside.

Frater pointed with a trembling finger.

I heard Thorpe draw a sharp breath, and Dr. Sprague swore aloud in amazement. Only Voorhies looked from one to another of us in dumb perplexity.

As for Mrs. Bewley, she emitted the shrill scream of a steam-whistle, and collapsed heavily against the deputy marshal. From his bewildered grasp she lifted a face yellow and twitching with fright.

"Is—is he down there?" she asked through chattering teeth. I managed to nod stiffly.

It took a clergyman to master his primitive fear quickly and take command of the situation.

"Mrs. Bewley," Thorpe said sternly, "you answered me blasphemously last evening that only a miracle could make you change your mind and cease your persecution of this good man.

"The miracle has occurred. I expect you to leave at once, taking this officer with you, and withdraw your petition for an injunction against your fellow-directors. Alpheus Morgan is to rest here in peace. And you are to make no reprisals against his friends, who have seen to it that his express wish was obeyed.

"Is that understood?"

In our unbelieving sight Floretta Bewley bent her arrogant head, turned meekly, and tottered shakily, supported by Voorhies, back to her car.

Because—she had seen what we all had seen.

Everywhere else in that wilderness of death last night's snow was piled heavily on mounds and tombstones. But at Old Man Morgan's grave, instead of the huge, clumsily piled mass of earth we had left behind us, the ground had been smoothed level, with four straight edges defining it. Only the few flakes still falling spotted its uniform brown.

And around it, in the heavy snow, were no footsteps whatever.

MRS. HINCK

"I'd like an older, more settled woman if I could get one—somebody reliable," Gwen said into the telephone. "I've had high school girls and they invite their friends and play the phonograph all hours and keep the children awake. . . . Two, a boy eight and a girl five. . . . Oh, that would be fine. Could she come tomorrow at 6?"

Mrs. Hinck arrived promptly on the hour, a comfortable, grandmotherly sort of person. Gav and Ada seemed to take to her at once. Best of all, Dale wouldn't have to drive her home when they got back; she came in her own little two-seater, which she parked outside.

"Give the children their supper as soon as we leave," Gwen instructed her. "It's all ready in the kitchen. Ada's bedtime is 8 and Gav can stay up till half-past. He can take care of himself, but you'll have to help Ada a little. And oh, yes, much as we deplore it"—Gwen made a little *moue* and Mrs. Hinck smiled sympathetically—"there's a riproaring program on television that they won't be happy without. It comes on at 7:30."

"Now don't you worry about anything," said Mrs. Hinck competently. "We're going to get along beautifully."

It was after 1 when Gwen and Dale got home. The only light was in the living room, where Mrs. Hinck sat placidly knitting something in yellow wool. She had even cleaned up the children's supper dishes. Gwen breathed a sigh of relief, remembering the high school girls.

"It's after midnight, so we owe you an hour overtime," Dale said.

"Nonsense," responded Mrs. Hinck. "I always sit up late anyhow, and I'm just knitting here instead of at home."

Gwen and Dale exchanged incredulous glances.

"Would you have time to come often—say twice a week?" Gwen asked. She didn't want to be more specific till she found out how the kids had liked her. "I'll phone in the morning—what's your number?"

"I'm sorry, but I haven't any phone," said Mrs. Hinck apologetically. "Just call the agency—I check with them every day."

She folded the yellow wool into a knitting bag, put on her smart black hat and coat, and drove away.

"Well, kids, what happened to Roaring Roger last night?" Dale inquired genially at the breakfast table.

Gav and Ada stared at each other blankly.

"Well, for gosh sake!" Gav exploded. "We forgot all about him! Mrs. Hinck was telling us a story."

"Do you like her?"

"She's swell," they said in chorus.

It was grand, being able to get out again together. Gwen was a devoted mother, but you can't help being young and wanting a little fun sometimes. On Mrs. Hinck's second evening, they arranged for Wednesdays and Saturdays, regularly.

"And maybe an extra evening once in a while, if you're not too busy," Gwen said recklessly.

"Any time—just let the agency know. To tell the truth, this is all the baby-sitting I'm doing right now. But I'd love to come here whenever you say. I like children, and I get so lonesome for my own little granddaughter. This is a sweater for her that I'm knitting."

"How old is she?" Gwen asked.

"Just about a year older than your Ada. I miss her a lot."

"Isn't she here in the city?"

"Oh, no, my daughter lives abroad. She married a foreigner: Illinck is his name. I was with them for a while, but I don't know when I'll go back. I just got the wanderlust in my old age, and decided to travel, and now I seem to have settled down here. I do miss Mary, though—and my daughter too, of course. I guess Mary misses me too. She's an only child, and there are no other children around. I wish she had your little boy and girl to play with. They're lovely youngsters."

"We think so," Dale grinned. "Thanks a lot, incidentally, for weaning them from that blood-and-thunder TV program. How did you do it?"

"Oh, I just tell them stories," Mrs. Hinck said vaguely. "I guess they just get interested and forget the television. I did the same way with Mary when I was there. They don't have television, but it was the same thing with radio."

"Illinck," Dale remarked after Mrs. Hinck had left. "That's a funny name—wonder what nationality he is?"

"I can't imagine. Don't let's ask any questions, Dale, there might be some family trouble. I noticed she didn't want to say much. And we don't want to offend her and lose her—we're too lucky."

"*I'm* the one that's lucky," Dale retorted, "getting a chance again to go places with my best girl."

Nevertheless, Gwen couldn't avoid a tiny unworthy twinge of jealousy when Gav and Ada began watching from the front window for Mrs. Hinck, and rushing to the door to greet her with hugs.

"Don't be a goof," she admonished herself. "She isn't stealing your kids' affections—they're as fond of us as ever. They just needed a grandmother, and she needed some grandchildren."

On summer evenings when it was still light after dinner and they weren't going anywhere, Dale would cut the grass or water the front garden while Gwen got rid of the dishes. That was the signal for Gav and Ada to perch on the bottom step of the porch and engage him in conversation.

"Daddy, why don't I have a grandmother?" That was Ada.

"You have—you've got two of them, and two grandfathers too, only they live way off at the other end of the country. They send you Christmas and birthday presents—don't you remember? Maybe some day one of them will visit us."

"Whenever Mrs. Hinck goes to visit her granddaughter, she takes her simply wonderful toys," said Ada wistfully.

"Well, if one of your grandmothers comes to see you, she'll bring you toys, too."

"Not like Mrs. Hinck," Ada objected stubbornly. "Mrs. Hinck brings Mary toys like nobody else in the world has—she told us so."

"Pig," remarked Gav. "Hey, daddy, can I hold the hose for a while now, huh?"

"I'm getting a trifle tired of Mrs. Hinck's little granddaughter," Dale commented later to Gwen. "She must be the worst spoiled brat in creation."

"She does seem kind of hipped on the subject, doesn't she? But she's lonely, I guess, poor old thing."

"Just so she doesn't give our kids grandiose ideas. Toys like none in the whole world—gosh!"

Another evening, and another gardening session.

"When Mrs. Hinck visits her granddaughter," said Gav informatively, "she doesn't use a train or a bus or a ship or a plane to get there."

"That's nice. What does she do—walk and swim?"

"No, she just *goes.*"

Curiosity overmastered Dale.

"She ever tell you the name of the country where her granddaughter lives?"

"Sure. It's called America, just like this one."

"America, eh? And what language do they speak there?"

"Why, English, just like us, of course."

Dale felt ashamed of his prying. Mrs. Hinck obviously had forestalled any possible inquiries on his or Gwen's part. He changed the subject.

"How's your granddaughter's sweater coming along?" Gwen asked Mrs. Hinck the next time she came.

"Almost done. I'm going to make a cap to match. It's for her seventh birthday. Some time this fall I might just pop over and visit there—I do miss Mary so much. How I wish I could take your two along! It would be wonderful for Mary."

"Yes, it's too bad it's so far away," Gwen answered absent-mindedly. Her heart sank. There would never be another Mrs. Hinck, and she and Dale had been having such good times together. "But you'd be back, wouldn't you?" she asked hopefully.

"Oh, I think so, unless—well, anyway, we needn't think about it yet."

That was in August. On Saturday night in the first week of October Dale and Gwen went to a party they hated to be the first ones to break up. It was after 3 when they drove up to their door.

"I feel guilty, keeping that poor old lady up so late," Gwen murmured.

"She's gone to sleep, I guess," Dale consoled her. "There's no light in the living room."

Gwen let out a startled cry.

"Dale!" she gasped. "Look—her car isn't here. She *couldn't* have gone home and left the children alone in the house—not Mrs. Hinck!"

They raced in. There was no one in the living room or anywhere else on the first floor. Together they ran upstairs, the same sudden terror in their hearts.

The two little bedrooms were dark, and the beds were empty. They had not been slept in.

Gwen's knees failed her. Dale dashed to the phone to call the police.

"Gwen," he shouted back from the hall, "what's the license number of Mrs. Hinck's car? I never noticed."

"I never did either," Gwen quavered.

It was almost dawn—with Gwen in tears and Dale pacing the floor—before the police called back. They'd found the license number at last, from the records, and they'd sent a man to the address Mrs. Hinck had given as hers. It was an all-night parking lot.

The night man there knew Mrs. Hinck by sight, but he hadn't seen her since he came on duty at 8. She kept her car there all the time, paying by the month; that was all he knew.

The whole long day was a nightmare. Neither of them had slept, and they kept going on black coffee, for they couldn't eat. A detective had appeared early in the morning and looked at the children's rooms. Nothing of theirs or of their parents' was missing, and there were no signs of struggle, or any evidence that a disturber had been there.

"They were kidnaped, all right," the detective concluded. "But they must have gone voluntarily."

What does "voluntarily" mean, when it is applied to children of five and eight?

Dale told him about the daughter who had married a foreigner named Illinck and lived abroad.

"Never heard of such a name," said the detective. "That all you know about him? We'll send out a general alarm right away, of course, but I don't see how she could leave the country without a passport." He took out his notebook. "Now give me a full description of the little girl and boy. And this Mrs. Hinck—what does she look like?"

"About five feet five, rather plump, nicely curled white hair, bifocals in a gold frame."

It sounded like the description of half the grandmothers in the world.

"Well, that helps a lot," said the detective with false encouragement. "No ransom note, I suppose, or anything like that?"

"No, nothing at all."

"And there won't be, I'm sure of that," Dale put in. "This isn't a kidnapping for money; the old lady seemed to be very well off. It's more like—well, the way I figure it out, she grew fond of our kids and that's why she took them."

"We get plenty of cases like that, though it's usually younger women. By the way, we've checked with the manager of the agency you got her from. They don't know a thing about her. She just came in there and signed up one day. They sent her out half a dozen times but she didn't seem to like the people and wouldn't go to any of them again, till they sent her to you. And the only address she gave was what turned out to be that parking lot."

"I'm absolutely positive," Gwen insisted, "that she's gone to her daughter and granddaughter, and taken Gav and Ada with her. She told me she might make a visit to them this fall, and she said something, months ago, about wishing she could take our two along with her. I thought she was just talking. And of course I expected she'd tell us ahead of time when she planned to leave."

"Neither did you think she'd snatch your children when she went, naturally. Well, folks, don't lose heart. I have kids of my own, and I know how you feel. But we're on the job, and we'll stay on it. We ought to have results very soon. From what you've told me, there isn't a chance she'd do any harm to them. And if she makes any attempt to spirit them out of the country—"

"Oh, the secret journey! I just remembered. Gav said to me only yesterday, 'Mrs. Hinck says some day she'll take us on a secret journey to a strange place.' I just laughed—I never even thought—"

"The only strange place she's going to see is the inside of a jail," the detective said.

But day passed into night again, and still there was no word of progress. They had tried again to eat but the food choked them. Finally they did drop asleep for an hour or two in the late afternoon, until the phone shocked them awake. But it was only the detective, to say that Mrs. Hinck's car had been found parked in the driveway of a vacant house at the other end of the city.

Husband and wife stood together at the front window where Gav and Ada had stood so often watching for Mrs. Hinck. They had stood there for a long time, not even bothering to turn on the lights as night came on. Dale held Gwen close to him, and once in a while she wept quietly.

"Look, darling," he said at last gently. "Are you thinking what I'm thinking?"

Gwen lifted a wet face and nodded dumbly. Her lips trembled.

"I felt you were. Looking out here reminded me of things the kids used to talk about to me while I gardened.

"Gwen, you never studied any foreign languages: I did. *Hinc* means *on this side* in Latin, and *illinc* means *from that side.*"

Gwen found a shaky voice.

"And the thing you told me, that Gav said—when Mrs. Hinck goes to visit her granddaughter—"

"She doesn't take a train or a bus or a ship or a plane—she just *goes.* Yes, that too."

"Oh, Dale! there were so many hints we never even noticed. That country's America, too, and the language they speak is English."

"We thought that was funny, or just to keep us from snooping. We'd better face it, Gwen. If we're right, the police can't ever get them back to us. And Mrs. Hinck won't need any passport where she's taken them."

She started to sob again. Dale held her tightly, his own face twisted.

" 'I wish she had your little boy and girl to play with'!" he quoted bitterly.

"The toys!" Gwen whispered. "The toys that are simply wonderful, that aren't like any others in the world—"

GONE TO THE DOGS

What woke Lida was being hit on the nose with a pajama button. She opened her eyes abruptly. It was just barely light. She turned sleepily, took one look at the other side of the double bed and let out a screech. The thing lying there opened its eyes—Henry's eyes—and said—in Henry's voice—"What's the matter, honey?"

It wasn't Henry, though. It was a Great Dane in Henry's pajamas, with the top buttons popped off by its barrel chest.

Lida shot out of bed. She got as far as the door before it occurred to her that she might be the one who had gone crazy. Trembling, she inched back and took another look.

It was a Great Dane, all right.

"I—I—you look like a dog!" she managed to gasp.

Henry—or whatever was there—took it calmly. Henry always took everything calmly.

"Are you just calling me a sonofabitch in a nice way, or is something wrong with your eyes?"

Lida made a tremendous effort and pulled herself together. Ordinarily she was almost as calm as Henry.

"It isn't my eyes," she breathed. "Either I've lost my mind or something awful has happened to you. Look at yourself—uh—Henry, and tell me which it is."

Henry's myopic blue eyes inspected his arm—his foreleg—well, his upper limb.

"Can't see a thing without my glasses. Give them to me, honey.

Something does feel funny. Bring me your hand-mirror, too."

The glasses wouldn't go on Henry's new broad nose. Lida held them with one shaking hand and passed over the mirror with the other. There was a long silence.

"You're not crazy, Lida," Henry said at last. "Something's happened."

Lida was speechless. Even Henry was shaken. He didn't drop the mirror, but he laid it down with a distinct thump. Perhaps that was because he had been holding it in the crook of his—limb. He no longer had an opposable thumb with which to grasp it. Unquestionably, what he now had was a large dog's paw.

"Shades of Kafka!" he said in an awed tone. "Thank God, I didn't turn into a giant cockroach!"

"B-but what—"

"How do I know? Things do happen. I've been trying for years to get you to take Charles Fort seriously. He has records of stranger things than this."

Lida burst into tears.

"Now don't cry, honey," He put out a comforting paw, but she shrank from it involuntarily. Fortunately for his feelings, Henry didn't see that. His glasses had fallen off as soon as she let go of them.

"We'll have to figure things out and use our common sense," he said in the reasonable tone she had been listening to for eight years.

"C-common sense! What has common sense to do with this unbelievable, horrible—"

"Hysteria won't help. Horrible maybe, but not unbelievable because it has happened—and when a thing is real, we have to believe it."

He climbed laboriously out from under the bedclothes, hesitated a moment, his hind paws hovering over his slippers, then stood solidly on all fours. The pajama pants fell down. Solemnly he peered at himself in Lida's full-length pier glass.

"I can't get a good look this way. Find some adhesive tape and fasten my glasses on for me, will you, Lida? And take this pajama top off me. It's—it's inappropriate."

In a waking nightmare, Lida did as she was told. Henry took a long look.

"A Great Dane!" he murmured. "I wonder why. I never cared for them particularly. They cost too much to feed. Well, let's get down to cases."

He glanced helplessly at the pad and pencil which always stood on the night table on his side of the bed. Until this morning, Henry Martindale had been a reasonably prosperous radio and television script writer.

"I can't think without notes, Lida," he sighed. "Write down what I tell you and I'll try to reason this thing out. But put on your dressing-gown first, dear, or you'll freeze."

This evidence of husbandly concern transformed Lida's horror into passionate loyalty and love. Somewhere within this canine shape, her own Henry lived intact. Suppose it had happened to her instead? Suppose she had awakened to find herself a Pekinese or a Siamese cat or a parakeet? Could she doubt that Henry would have stood by her?

She reached for her dressing-gown, wrapped herself in it and took up the pad and pencil.

At his dictation, she began to write the first considered reflections of Henry Martindale, Great Dane.

"One," he began, "this is either temporary or permanent. If it is temporary, I may wake up as myself tomorrow morning. In any event, I can manage to wait for a week—with your cooperation, Lida—" She nodded and even contrived to smile. "For a week, without arousing suspicion. Call up everybody we had engagements with and tell them I have the flu. Tell Mrs. Whoozis the same thing when she comes to clean, and keep her out of this room. I have a deadline on that story for Channel Twenty, but I can dictate it as usual and you can deliver it. You'd better do all the phoning, too. I could talk, but I doubt if I could hold the phone."

Lida hid her shudder. Henry went on dictating.

"Two—if this condition is permanent, if it isn't gone in a week or so, then it may mean that I must face my remaining life-span as a Great Dane. Question—have I now the life-expectancy of a human being or of a dog?

"I must then make a major decision: where and how can I live? I have earned my living for fifteen years now as a writer. I could continue to dictate my stories, of course, but it would be utterly impossible to conceal my—my present appearance. It would be still more impossible to explain it, even to such hardened sophisticates as the script editors and agency men for whom I write. As for the family—my brother and Aunt Agatha and your mother, Lida, and the rest of your relatives—I could, perhaps, brazen it out and make advantageous connections with a television program."

"I won't have that!" Lida burst out hotly. "I won't have you displaying yourself as a—as a freak!"

"An intelligent talking dog might be worth big money to the right sponsor," Henry said reasonably.

"No. They'd investigate first and—you couldn't get away with it anyway, Henry. Your eyes—they're still yours and people would wonder. And your voice—you've talked too often in public and on the air. Winchell would be sure to scent something and then all the other columnists would take it up."

"Perhaps you're right—it might be too risky—even though it would have been rather fun. Well, then, if I'm stuck for an indefinite period with this—this phenomenon, there will be only one thing I can do. We must go somewhere where we know nobody, where you can be a widow who lives alone with only her dog for company." He paused. "Wait a moment, Lida. No, don't write this down. Maybe I'm assuming too much. I'm taking it for granted that you'll be with me. No, let me finish. If you feel you can't stand it—if you want to go away, I'll understand—I'd never blame you. And, Lida, I beg of you, don't stick by me out of a sense of duty, just because a dog without an owner—even a dog that can think and talk—is a lost dog. Just because . . ."

He had to stop. His throat had tightened too much for him to go on.

Lida's last vestige of horror left her. "Don't be a fool, darling," she said brusquely. "I married you, not your looks. *You're* still here. If we have to go to the ends of the earth—if I have to pretend forever that you're my pet Great Dane . . ." She gulped down a sob. "Just so we're together . . ."

"Bless you, dearest," Henry said quietly. He had recovered his usual calm. "Go on taking this down now. We won't have to go to the ends of the earth. We can find some secluded place in the country, perhaps not more than a hundred miles from here. We'll have to think of ways to fend off our families and friends. But I can dictate my stories to you and we can handle all my business contacts by mail. There will be difficulties, of course. How can I sign letters or endorse checks, for instance?"

"I can forge your signature. I've done it before on letters, when you were deep in a story and didn't want to be disturbed."

"Yes, that would work. And we'll find means to solve the other problems as they come up. All we need face now is a week of waiting to see if this—transformation is permanent."

A thought occurred to Lida. "About food, Henry." she suggested nervously. "Do you want to eat as usual or—or should I buy some Canine Delight?"

"Hm—that's a point." Henry let his mind dwell on ham and eggs, then on Canine Delight. "I'm sorry, dear," he said apologetically, "but I'm afraid you'd better lay in a supply of dog food."

"It's eight o'clock. The grocery at the corner will be open. I'll dress and go out to get some—some breakfast for you. And here—I'll fasten your glasses on firmly so you can read the paper while I'm gone."

Already, she discovered gratefully, she was becoming accustomed to the new Henry. Her hands were steady as she adjusted the tape. She restrained an impulse to stroke the tawny head.

Henry watched her leave, his large myopic blue eyes moist. He had not mentioned the fear that gnawed at him, a fear worse than the bite of hunger. Suppose this were an intermediate stage—suppose he should gradually become more dog and less man, lose his power of speech, his power of human thought?

Time enough to face that if it began to happen. Time, probably, to run away alone into the unknown before she could stop him. Fortunately, all they possessed was in their joint names and ultimately Lida would have to let him be declared dead and cash in on his sizable insurance.

He gazed unseeingly at the paper most of the time while she was gone. Nothing in it was as strange as what had happened to Henry Martindale.

The week went by somehow. Every night Henry went to sleep a Great Dane—he admitted he was more comfortable sleeping on a rug beside the bed—and every morning he woke up a Great Dane again. He ate Canine Delight and one night when Lida broiled two chops for herself, he enjoyed the juicy bones. But he felt no impulse to wag his tail or to bark. Inside, he was still completely Henry.

They devised a strap to hold his spectacles on, to avoid the pulling of hair that accompanied removing the adhesive tape. Physically, he was comfortable, though he began to long for exercise and fresh air. He could stand anything for a week—even Aunt Agatha's insistence that she must come to help nurse the poor boy, plus her resentment of Lida's firm refusal. Once there was a scare when the woman who came twice a week to clean insisted that she could vacuum the bedroom without bothering the invalid—but Lida won that round.

At the end of the week, it became obvious that the metamorphosis was either permanent or would be of indefinite duration. Henry had met his deadline and dictated the beginning of another story in his television series, but he felt distracted and uninterested.

"I guess this is it, Lida," he conceded on the eighth day. "We have to plan."

They pored over maps and made a list of upstate villages to be inspected.

"I can make the trips and come back and report to you," said Lida dubiously. "But I hate to leave you here all alone day after day. You could let the phone ring, but suppose Aunt Agatha came or Bill Goodlett or the Harrisons? Or a telegram or a special delivery letter?"

"I'll go with you," Henry decided promptly. "Call up all the likely people and tell them I'm better, but you're taking me to the country to recuperate. We'll write everybody later, when we've found a place, that we're going to stay for a while. But first you'd better buy me a dog-collar and a leash, and then take me downtown and get a license for me."

"Oh, *darling!*"

"I know—it's grim. But we must be practical. I'll have to have a name, too. What do you want to call your Great Dane? Anything but Hamlet will suit me."

"Why can't you still be Henry?" asked Lida faintly.

"Well, I guess it wouldn't matter—where we're going, wherever that is, they wouldn't get the point. All right, register me as Henry. I'll sit in the back of the car, as a dog should. Thank goodness you can drive, honey. I'd hate to travel in a baggage car!"

So Lida, her huge dog in the back seat, began visiting rural real estate offices to inquire about secluded cottages for rent. There was no sense in tying up their capital by buying a house, when at any moment—as they still assured each other—this calamity might end and Henry be himself again.

All they got was turndowns. There was nothing, simply nothing, to be had. Villagers, they learned, don't rent their homes.

They had reached a state of dull despair when, almost the last on their hopeful list, they drove to Farmington.

Yes, said Mr. Bullis, there *was* one place—the old Gassingham house. It was in kinda bad shape, needed some work done and it was three miles from the highway. But Liz Gassingham—she was all that was left—she lived in town now and she refused to sell. She'd never said she'd rent, but she might.

Lida almost said she would take it sight unseen, but stopped herself in time.

"There's only one thing, Mrs. Martindale. That dog of yours . . ." He cast an unfriendly eye on Henry, lying peaceably on the floor of the real estate office.

"You mean Miss Gassingham wouldn't let me keep a pet?"

"Pet, yes—but pets to Liz is cats. She mightn't like the idea of a tenant with a dog—a monster dog like that, especially."

"But, Mr. Bullis, I told you—I'm all alone since my husband—went . . ." Lida's voice shook. "The doctor said I must go to the country to get back my strength. But I'd be afraid to live so far from people without Henry to protect me."

"That his name, Henry?"

Henry laid a warning paw on her foot. They had agreed that they must keep their own name because of the mail and she was remembering that most of the letters would be addressed to Henry.

"It's silly—perhaps you'll think it's crazy—but that was my husband's name. I—it makes me feel less lonely to call the dog Henry, too. He—went so so suddenly."

"Um." Mr. Bullis sounded disapproving. "Well, let's go see

Liz. Put the mutt in your car. You might talk her over, but not if she saw him first. Funny-looking dog at that, if you don't mind my saying so—awful funny-looking eyes. Will he make a row if you leave him?"

"Oh, no, Henry never—Great Danes don't bark much."

"Better lock him in. If the kids spot him, they'll be all over him and you don't want him jumping out."

Henry settled down philosophically in the car and took a nap.

Lida came back triumphant.

"I told her you were a settled old dog, Henry, too lazy to do any damage," she announced. "And that you were clean and never had fleas and just loved cats."

"Good gosh!" said Mr. Bullis, staring. "You talk to that mutt just like he was human!"

Lida tried to smile it off. "That's what being alone does to people, Mr. Bullis."

The house was pretty dreadful. It was big and watertight, but that was about all that could be said for it. Their modern furniture would look weird in it. The only lighting was by kerosene lamps. The water came from an outdoor pump—Henry wondered dismally if he could learn to pump with his mouth. The sanitary arrangements consisted of a Chick Sale in the back yard, and the cooking had to be done on a wood stove, with a fireplace for central heating.

But they had to have it and they could get along somehow. At least, Mr. Bullis said, Lida could hire Ed Monahan to chop wood and do the heaviest chores and there was old Mrs. Sharp—she sometimes took in washing for the summer people and she might be willing to do Mrs. Martindale's household laundry. He looked disparagingly at Lida's city-bred slenderness.

A month later, all the lies had been told, all the arrangements had been made and Lida and Henry were residents of Farmington.

It was pretty rugged. Henry had to be careful—and make sure his spectacles were off—whenever anyone came to the house. But they managed. His mind had never been working better and he dictated scripts like mad, till he had a good backlog in several agency inventories. Smith, of D. D. B. & I., wrote him that if rusticating for their health would add the same touch of originality and conviction to other writers' stuff, he'd recommend it to all his regulars. Henry twitched his ears irascibly when he read that one.

In a way, it was Lida who unwittingly brought on the inevitable crisis.

It was an evening in early November. She was sitting by the fireplace, knitting a sweater for Henry, who was lying contentedly at her feet. Henry had become almost reconciled to being a dog. It was nice not having to wear clothes, for instance, though when the really cold weather came, he would probably want the sweater. He wished he could help Lida more with the housework, but there aren't many household tasks that can be done without hands.

Suddenly Lida said, "Henry, I've been thinking."

"So I've noticed. What about?" he countered.

"I've been thinking about—it."

"*It*" was what they had tacitly agreed to call Henry's transmogrification.

"What's the use of thinking about it?"

"That's just what I mean. You're just taking it lying down."

Henry rose to his feet and looked at her apologetically.

"Don't be silly," she said impatiently. "I don't mean that way. I mean you've—you've just accepted it. You haven't tried to—oh, to think how or why it happened or whether there's any way to undo it."

"Did the swan that was found in Central Park try to figure out how it could become Dorothy Arnold again?" Henry inquired sententiously.

"I don't know what you're talking about."

"Fort—I'm a Fortean phenomenon. He never said anything about the possibility of reversal."

"That doesn't mean it couldn't happen."

"Perhaps not. My guess is it would have to be spontaneous. But if it will make you any happier, Lida, I'll try anything you suggest."

"Henry, don't you *want* to be human again?"

"Because *you're* human, yes. But selfishly, I confess, so long as I have the mind and the power of speech of a human being . . ."

"That's one of the things I've been wondering about. A dog's throat and mouth aren't formed for human speech, yet you can talk clearly with your own voice."

"I know. I've been puzzled about that, too. And my sight—dogs haven't very good sight, anyway, so that might fit. But they're supposed to be color-blind and I'm not any more than I ever was. I know very well that sweater you're knitting is beige and maroon."

"What about your other senses?"

"Well, I always had keen hearing and I still have. But I certainly don't have the sense of smell of a dog—of other dogs, I mean."

"Don't say that!"

"I'm sorry. I get sort of confused sometimes. And there are other—disadvantages, of course. But, Lida, there's no use in going into all that. I don't know how to change it."

"Tell me, can you remember anything special about that night—the night before it happened?"

"I've tried. I remember I was working late on a script. It was nearly two when I went to bed and you were sound asleep. The last thing I recall was thinking, 'I'm dog-tired.' And then you woke me and it was morning and I was—like this."

"Dog-tired. Do you think . . ."

"Nonsense—pure coincidence. Or maybe . . ."

Henry felt sudden excitement thrill through him from head to tail. All his calm acceptance dropped from him as his pajamas once had done.

"Lida, I've just remembered! The story I was working on that night was the one about a werewolf who evolved from a primitive wolflike creature instead of from apes, as we did."

Lida stared at him. "You mean . . ."

"Could be. Perhaps that story wasn't just imaginary—perhaps I happened on actual facts and got transformed as a warning, maybe, or maybe that's how people turn into werewolves."

"Then there might be a way for you to change back again!"

"I don't see how. I didn't engineer it and I wouldn't know how to engineer the reversal. I'd have to get in touch somehow with a real werewolf. Hey, here's an idea! Let's get to work on another story about werewolves. It might be like—like tuning them in, if they really exist. And perhaps my transformer would get on my beam again. He might be glad to straighten me out."

"But suppose he isn't. *You're* not altogether sorry about being a dog—you just told me so. Suppose he decides you *like* being a pet, with no responsibilities."

"That's not fair, honey." Henry's tone was aggrieved. "Don't I work just as hard as I ever did?"

"Oh, darling, I didn't mean you—just him!"

"In that case, he won't want to change me back and everything will stay the way it is now. What else could he do to me?"

Henry began dictating the new werewolf script the next morning. It went fast and smoothly, as if something in him knew beforehand what to say.

Yet neither of them felt comfortable. He said nothing to Lida, but under the flow of words he was conscious of an inner struggle, as if something or somebody were trying vainly to impede them. And she, though the original incitement had been her own, grew increasingly nervous and apprehensive.

At the end of three hours, the script was half done and both of them were exhausted.

"Let's knock off for the rest of the day," Henry suggested. "We can go on with it tomorrow. We both need exercise. I'd like to explore those thick woods—the ones we've never gone into."

Nothing could have been more trim, tame and civilized than Farmington. Yet not five miles from the village, in the back country, lay the last remnants of what was once virgin forest. Its trees were of no value as timber and it had a bad reputation. There were said to be wildcats there, even bears. Parts of it belonged to landowners who never bothered with it, parts were still in the public domain. Local stories made it the hideout of robbers in the past and children were disciplined by threats of taking them there and leaving them.

Lida took Henry's spectacles off him and put on his collar and leash. Passing through the village in the car, they encountered Liz Gassingham, who scarcely returned Lida's greeting and snorted at sight of Henry.

"Great, horrible thing!" she muttered, glaring. "If she ever lets it loose to hurt my kitties, I'll throw her out, lease or no lease!"

They parked the car at the end of the road and walked half a mile over fields to the edge of the wood. Once inside, Lida shrank back a little.

"Henry," she said, "do you think there really are wild animals here? Let's not go too far."

Henry couldn't smile any more, but he laid a protecting paw on her hand. "The Great Dane," he said soothingly, "was originally a boarhound. I can handle anything we're likely to meet. And we won't get lost—don't forget I have the canine sense of direction. I can't explain it, Lida, but all day I've felt impelled toward these woods," he added.

"Maybe something *is* going to happen here," said Lida hopefully. "Oh, darling, if it only would! You do want it, too, don't you?"

"I want us to be alike again, dearest."

They walked for an hour among the old trees and Henry ran eagerly from tree to tree, sniffing. They startled woodchucks and squirrels, but nothing larger appeared. It was very quiet and peaceful and not too cold, even with the trees bare and patches of early snow left here and there on the ground from the first fall of the season. After a while, they found themselves climbing until the level floor of the woods had become a hill.

Suddenly Henry darted through some underbrush toward a depression in the hillside, behind the bulk of a huge uprooted tree.

"You know," he called back in a voice that shook a little, "this could be dug out to make a good snug cave. I could do it myself with my paws."

"What of it? You don't want to live in a cave, do you?"

"I suppose not." The excitement deserted him. "I'm all confused. There was something very important I was thinking about and now I seem to have forgotten it completely."

"Poor Henry, you're tired. Let's go back. I'm tired, too."

"I guess it was all nonsense about werewolves, after all," said Henry in the car. "Well, it's a pretty good story, anyway. The agency ought to eat it up. You know, darling, I just remembered—vampires turn people they bite into their own kind. Why not werewolves?"

"But you're a weredog," said Lida absently. Then, sharply, "Henry, you wouldn't!"

When rent day came around, Lida didn't turn up at Liz Gassingham's house.

Mrs. Sharp had a whole washing ready that Lida never called for.

Ed Monahan went out to chop wood, but found nobody home.

Mail piled up in the post office and the postmistress noted, as so often before, that most of it was addressed to the deceased Mr. Martindale. Why, she wondered loudly, didn't the woman tell his friends he had passed away—or deserted her, more likely? Something funny there!

But nobody moves fast in Farmington and over a week passed before a delegation, led by Mr. Bullis, went out to investigate.

The door was unlocked and the house was empty.

Everything was in order, with the table laid for breakfast and the stove stuffed with wood and paper, ready to light.

The bed had been slept in and at its foot, where apparently that dog slept on a rug, lay a white flannel nightgown frivolously printed with sprigs of roses. All its buttons were off.

The rest of Lida's usual house attire lay over the back of a chair. Her shoes were beneath it, a pair of pink bedroom slippers beside the bed.

It was a year from the following summer that two adventurous boys from the village, egging each other on, raided the big woods. They came back, pale and frightened, to report that they had seen the dog that used to belong to Mrs. Martindale. It had emerged from the thick underbrush, they said, where the slope of the ground began to climb the hill. It had gone back to the wild, the boys claimed, and they had been lucky to get away without harm.

"You might have been killed. Somebody ought to go out there and shoot the thing." Mr. Bullis asserted.

"Aw," said the older of the two, aged fifteen, looking a bit sick, "it wasn't doing nobody no hurt. Nobody hardly ever goes there anyhow. I know *I* ain't going no more."

"There was a she-dog too, just like him, and some puppies," the younger boy blurted out.

"Shut up!" growled the older. "You want folks to think you're crazy? Jim was so scared, he got to seeing things, Mr. Bullis. There wasn't nothing there 'cept that big mutt of Mrs. Martindale's."

"I wasn't scared," Jim retorted. He caught his friend's eye and added hastily, "But I could of made a mistake."

"You must have, my boy," said Mr. Bullis kindly. "That dog was a Great Dane and there's never been another anywhere around here that I ever heard of."

"You idiot!" The fifteen-year-old scolded when the two boys were alone again. "Don't you ever open your yap about that again. They'd put us both in the booby-hatch."

They kept far away from the woods after that and gradually they became convinced that they must have been out of their heads for a while. How *could* a dog have yelled, "Scram, you kids, or do you want me to bite?"

THE MARGENES

There is a small striped smelt called the grunion which has odd egglaying habits. At high tide, on the second, third, and fourth nights after the full of the moon from March to June, thousands of female grunions ride in on the waves to a beach in southern California near San Diego, dig tail-first into the soft sand, deposit their eggs, then ride back on the wash of the next wave. The whole operation lasts about six seconds.

On the nights when the grunion are running, hordes of people used to come to the beach with baskets and other containers, and with torches to light the scene, and try to catch the elusive little fish in their hands.

They were doing that on an April night in 1980. In the midst of the excitement of the chase, only a few of them noticed that something else was riding the waves in with the grunions.

Among the few who stopped grunion-catching long enough to investigate were a girl named Marge Hickin and a boy named Gene Towanda. They were UCLA students, "going together," who had come down on Saturday from Los Angeles for the fun.

"What on earth do you think these can be, Gene?" Marge asked, holding out on her palms three or four of the little circular, wriggling objects, looking like small-size doughnuts, pale straw in color.

"Never saw anything like them," Gene admitted. "But then my major's psychology, not zoology. They don't seem to bite, anyway. Here let's collect some of them instead of the fish. That dingus of yours will hold water. We can take them to the marine biology lab Monday and find out what they are."

Marge Hickin and Gene Towanda had started a world-wide economic revolution.

None of the scientists at the university laboratory knew what the little live straw-colored circles were, either. In fact, after a preliminary study they wouldn't say positively whether the creatures were animal or vegetable; they displayed voluntary movement, but they seemed to have no respiratory or digestive organs. They were completely anomalous.

The grunion ran again that night, and Gene and Marge stayed down to help the laboratory assistants gather several hundred of the strange new objects for further study. They were so numerous that they were swamping the fish, and the crowds at the beach began to grumble that their sport was being spoiled.

Next night the grunion stopped running—but the little doughnuts didn't. They never stopped. They came in by hundreds of thousands every night, and those that nobody gathered wriggled their way over the land until some of them even turned up on the highways (where a lot of them were smashed by automobiles), on the streets and sidewalks of La Jolla, and as far north as Oceanside and as far south as downtown San Diego itself.

The things were becoming a pest. There were indignant letters to the papers, and editorials were written calling on the authorities to do something. Just what to do, nobody knew; the only way to kill the circular little objects from the sea seemed to be to crush them—and they were too abundant for that to be very effective.

Meanwhile, the laboratory kept studying them.

Marge and Gene were interested enough to come down again the next weekend to find out what, if anything, had been discovered. Not much had: but one of the biochemists at the laboratory casually mentioned that chemically the straw-colored circles seemed to be almost pure protein, with some carbohydrates and fats, and that apparently they contained all the essential vitamins.

College student that he was, Gene Towanda immediately swallowed one of the wriggling things down whole, as a joke.

It tickled a little, but that wasn't what caused the delighted amazement on his face.

"Gosh!" he exclaimed. "It's delicious!"

He swallowed another handful.

That was the beginning of the great *margene* industry.

It was an astute reporter, getting a feature story on the sensational new food find, who gave the creatures their name, in honor of the boy and girl who had first brought the things to the attention of the scientists. He dubbed them margenes, and margenes they remained.

"Dr. O. Y. Willard, director of the laboratory," his story said in part, "thinks the margenes may be the answer to the increasing and alarming problem of malnutrition, especially in undeveloped countries.

" 'For decades now,' he said, 'scientists have been worried by the growing gap between world population and world food facilities. Over-farming, climatic changes caused by erosion and deforestation, the encroachment of building areas on agricultural land, and above all the unrestricted growth of population, greatest in the very places where food is becoming scarcest and most expensive, have produced a situation where, if no remedy is found, starvation or semi-starvation may be the fate of half the Earth's people. The ultimate result would be the slow degeneration and death of the entire human race.

" 'Many remedies have been suggested,' Dr. Willard commented further. 'They range from compulsory birth control to the production of synthetic food, hydroponics, and the harvesting of plankton from the oceans. Each of these presents almost insuperable difficulties.

" 'The one ideal solution would be the discovery of some universal food that would be nourishing, very cheap, plentiful, tasty, and that would not violate the taboos of any people anywhere in the world. In the margenes we may have discovered that food.

" 'We don't know where the margenes came from,' the director went on to say, 'and we don't even know yet what they are, biologically speaking. What we do know is that they provide more energy per gram than any other edible product known to man, that everyone who has eaten them is enthusiastic about their taste, that they can be processed and distributed easily and cheaply, and that they are acceptable even to those who have religious or other objections to certain other foods, such as beef among the Hindus or pork among the Jews and Mohammedans.

" 'Even vegetarians can eat them,' Dr. Willard remarked, 'since they are decidedly not animal in nature. Neither, I may add, are they vegetable. They are a hitherto utterly unknown synthesis of chemical elements in living form. Their origin remains undiscovered.' "

Naturally, there was no thought of feeding people on raw margenes. Only a few isolated places in either hemisphere would have found live food agreeable. Experiment showed that the most satisfactory way to prepare them was to boil them alive, like crabs or lobsters. They could then be ground and pressed into cakes, cut into convenient portions. One one-inch-square cube made a nourishing and delicious meal for a sedentary adult, two for a man engaged in hard physical labor.

And they kept coming in from the Pacific Ocean nightly, by the million.

By this time none of them had to be swept off streets or highways. The beach where for nearly a century throngs had gathered for the sport of catching grunion was off bounds now; it was the property of California Margene, Inc., a private corporation heavily subsidized by the Federal Government as an infant industry. The grunions themselves had to find another place to lay their eggs, or die off—nobody cared which. The sand they had used for countless millennia as an incubator was hemmed in by factory buildings and trampled by margene-gatherers. The whole beautiful shore for miles around was devastated; the university had to move its marine biological laboratory elsewhere; La Jolla, once a delightful suburb and tourist attraction, had become a dirty, noisy honkytonk town where processing and cannery workers lived and spent their off-hours; the unique Torrey Pines had been chopped down because they interfered with the erection of a freight airport.

But half the world's people were living on margenes.

The sole possession of this wonderful foodstuff gave more power to the United States than had priority in the atomic bomb. Only behind the Iron Curtain did the product of California Margene, Inc. fail to penetrate. *Pravda* ran parallel articles on the same day, one claiming that margenes—*brzdichnoya*—had first appeared long ago on a beach of the Caspian Sea and had for years formed most of the Russian diet; the other, warning the deluded nations receiving free supplies as part of American foreign aid that the margenes had been injected with drugs aimed at making them weak and submissive to the exploitation of the capitalist-imperialists.

There was a dangerous moment at the beginning when the sudden sharp decline in stocks of all other food products threatened another 1929. But with federal aid a financial crash was averted and now a new high level of prosperity had been established. Technological unemployment was brief, and most of the displaced workers were soon retained for jobs in one of the many ramifications of the new margene industry.

Agriculture, of course, underwent a short deep depression, not only in America but all over the world; but it came to an end as food other than margenes quickly became a luxury product. Farmers were able to cut their production to a small fraction of the former yield, and to get rich on the dizzying prices offered for bread, apples, or potatoes. And this increased the prosperity of the baking and other related industries as well.

In fact, ordinary food costs (which meant margene costs) were so low that a number of the larger unions voluntarily asked for wage decreases in their next contracts. California Margene, Inc. was able to process, pack, and distribute margene cakes at an infinitesimal retail price, by reason of the magnitude of the output.

An era of political good feeling fell upon the western world, reflected from the well-fed comfort of vast populations whose members never before in their lives had had quite enough to eat. The fear of famine seemed to be over forever, and with it the fear of the diseases and the social unrest that follow famine. Even the U.S.S.R. and its satellites, in a conciliatory move in the United Nations Assembly, suggested that the long cold war ought to be amenable to a reasonable solution through a series of amicable discussions. The western nations, assenting, guessed shrewdly that the Iron Curtain countries "wanted in" on the margenes.

Marge Hickin and Gene Towanda, who had started it all, left college for copywriting jobs with the agency handling the enormous margene publicity; they were married a few months later.

And the margenes continued to come in from the sea in countless millions. They were being harvested now from the Pacific itself, near the shoreline, before they reached the beach. Still no research could discover their original source.

Only a few scientists worried about what would happen if the margenes should disappear as suddenly as they had arrived. Attempts at breeding the creatures had failed completely. They did not undergo fission, they did not sporulate, they seemed to have no sex. No methods of reproduction known in the plant or animal kingdom seemed to apply to them. Hundreds of them were kept alive for long periods—they lived with equal ease in either air or water, and they did not take nourishment, unless they absorbed it from their environment—but no sign of fertility ever appeared. Neither did they seem to die of natural causes. They just kept coming in . . .

On the night of May 7, 1989, not a single margene was visible in the ocean or on the beach.

They never came again.

What happened as a result is known to every student of history. The world-wide economic collapse, followed by the fall of the most stable governments, the huge riots that arose from the frantic attempts to get possession of the existing stocks of margene cakes or of the rare luxury items of other edibles, the announcement by the U.S.S.R. that it had known from the beginning the whole thing was a gigantic American hoax in the interests of the imperialistic bloodsuckers, the simultaneous atomic attacks by east and west, the Short War of 1990 that ruined most of what bombs had spared of the Earth, the slow struggle back of the remnant of civilization which is all of existence you and I have ever known—all these were a direct outgrowth of that first appearance of the margenes on the beach near San Diego on an April night in 1980.

Marge and Gene Towanda were divorced soon after they had both lost their jobs. She was killed in the hydrogen blast that wiped out San Diego; he fell in the War of 1990. "Margene" became a dirty word in every language on Earth. What small amount of money and ability can be spared is, as everyone knows, devoted today to a desperate international effort to reach and colonize another habitable planet of the Solar System, if such there be.

As for the margenes themselves, out of the untold millions that had come, only a few thousand were lucky enough to survive and find their way back to their overcrowded starting point. In their strange way of communication—as incomprehensible to us as would be their means of nourishment and reproduction, or their constitution itself—they made known to their kin what had happened to them. There is no possibility, in spite of the terrific over-population of their original home and of the others to which they are constantly migrating, that they will ever come here again.

There has been much speculation, particularly among writers of science fiction, on what would happen if aliens from other planets should invade Earth. Would they arrive as benefactors or as conquerors? Would we welcome them or would we overcome and capture them and put them in zoos and museums? Would we meet them in friendship or with hostility?

The margenes gave us the answer.

Beings from outer space came to Earth in 1980.

And we ate them.

THE OLD WOMAN

The façade of the All-Day branch of the largest bank in the world has wide sloping stone sills below its first-floor windows on the Willy Street side. Tired shoppers with heavy bundles find them convenient while they wait for a bus. Drunks use them to gather enough energy to stagger on to the nearest bar. And there are the regulars. There is a white-bearded man in a ragged overcoat who suns himself there on good days, having doubtless no other place to go except a dark hole of a room somewhere. There is a retired bus dispatcher who smokes a meditative pipe while he watches the traffic that no longer concerns him; once in a while a driver comes by who knew him in the old days and with whom he can exchange a greeting and feel for a minute that he isn't entirely outside of life, looking in.

And there was the Old Woman.

"It oughtn't to be allowed," said the young policeman indignantly. "She ought to be shut away."

"Why?" asked the experienced policeman who was showing him the beat on his first day. "She don't do no harm. She never bothers nobody. She don't even talk."

The Old Woman never spoke, even when spoken to. She was gaunt and dark-skinned with almost colorless hollow eyes. She was decently dressed and fairly clean, with a hat and a handbag and even gloves. She came every morning, rain or shine, except on Saturdays and Sundays when the bank was closed, and she sat there on the last sill at the west end of the building from eight in the morning to ten at night; the bank itself doesn't open till ten, but the safe-deposit vaults are open at eight.

All day long she sat there, beating her gloved hands about her, brushing something invisible from her face and body, waving her arms around in the air, quiet only in occasional moments of exhaustion.

Sometimes passers-by, usually housewifely looking women, would glance at her, become distressed and sympathetic, and go up to her. "Are you sick?" they would ask. "Can I help you?" She never answered. She never even looked at them. Somebody accustomed to the neighborhood would motion the inquirer away, tapping his forehead meaningly; or the good Samaritan would give up, perplexed and upset, and walk off, shaking her head. The Old Woman paid no attention.

Somewhere else, though, somebody noticed. Somebody sent a message. Somebody renewed the attack.

This thing had been going on now for sixteen years, ever since the Old Woman had refused orders to return home. It had been a losing battle, so far, against her indomitable will, but they never gave up. They never could. Things were going to pot because of the Old Woman's absence—only there she wasn't the Old Woman. But she had refused to listen to reason, cajolery and persuasion left her cold, she ignored commands. They hadn't the force to abduct her bodily. So they were doing the only thing left—harassing her almost beyond endurance, but not quite beyond it. That seemed to be failing too, but they had nothing else in their arsenal, so they kept at it.

And meanwhile, in that somewhere else, crops were failing, glaciers were encroaching on arable land, all because one obstinate creature insisted on staying where she was.

Why? She wouldn't even tell them that.

In baffled fury, they sent new swarms of invisible annoyers to torment her. She sat on the sill of the bank building and fought them off in silence, her face grim.

Of course she had a room where she spent her evenings and nights and weekends, where she ate and slept. She even had a name there, but only for the benefit of the landlord, and then only when she rented the place; after that, she sent him the exact rent every month in a plain envelope. She bought her food in supermarkets where no one knew her. She could talk well if she wanted to, but she never did; she needed to hoard her strength for the daily struggle. At home, at night, she was safe, for they could not get at her while her part of the earth was dark. Sometimes, sitting alone in her room, she permitted herself a pitying smile. They thought they could wear her down, did they? They seemed to have forgotten who and what she was.

And if they knew *why* she stayed all day just in that particular spot, how terrified they would be!

It came finally to a top-level, top-secret conference of all the most important and powerful of those concerned—all except, naturally, the Old Woman herself. While it went on, elsewhere and elsewhen, she was busy sitting on the stone sill and fighting off the invisible annoyers who made her days one long grisly battle.

"Has it something to do with the structure she haunts?" asked one. (Their names are unpronounceable, their offices and functions indescribable.) "And could we compel her, then, by destroying the entire structure?"

"We tried that once," replied a colleague gloomily, "and it failed. Without her own power we have not sufficient strength.

(The police were sure the abortive fire at the bank was set, but they could never discover the method and never found a trace of the arsonist.)

"But if we are able to get messages across, and even to send the *anwahs* regularly to attack her, why aren't we strong enough to take away whatever it is that keeps her there?"

"We might be, if we could find out what it is. But we don't even know that this is her reason. We don't know anything, because she won't tell us."

Impasse again. Then the youngest member had a bright idea.

"Could we kill her? There can be no successor as *mikuna* until she is dead."

They looked at him contempuously. Several of them wondered if it hadn't been a mistake to raise him to leadership.

"She took with her the tokens by which the new *mikuna* could be recognized," one of them explained at last. "Either she comes back, or we shall never have a *mikuna* again. And I suppose even you"—he couldn't resist that slur—"realize what that would mean."

"The end," moaned the assembled leaders. And even the youngest echoed, "The end."

"And we can't wait much longer," sighed the most venerable of them all. "My whole estate in the south is buried deep in mud from a flash flood." "And mine has become a dust bowl," agreed his nearest colleague.

If the Old Woman had wanted to bother, she had the means to listen in, and she might have derived some sardonic amusement from overhearing the discussion. But she was too busy fighting off *anwahs,* while she sat on the sill of the bank building.

There was no object whatever in the bank vaults that interested her. She stayed where she did, and haunted the building, and refused to go home, because of something that *wasn't* there.

She was waiting for it. She would know.

She was the ninth *mikuna* of her line. She had been recognized and installed when she was only eight years old. That was 211 years ago. She was ripe with experience and wisdom and power.

She had not deserted her home, or refused to return to it, out of any dissatisfaction or anger. She had gone, and she remained, because only so could she save it from utter disaster.

There was no guarantee that she could save it. If she must stay much longer, it might be destroyed in another manner, because of her absence alone. But that risk was the only chance. And she could not have waited to explain, or the chance might have been lost.

Sixteen years ago, laying her plots for the annual prophecy, she had learned the shocking future. There was only one way to avert it, and that way she had taken, at once. It was her responsibility. She alone was their guardian and preserver.

There was a star so far away and insignificant that it had no name, only a number, in their astronomy. Around it eight planets revolved. On one of them—on a particular spot on one of them—within a particular artifact of its inhabitants, a creature of the planet's dominant breed so like and so unlike her own would one day place an object which, if it were not wrested from him, would spell the doom of her own world. (Of others too, but she did not care about that.) He must be anticipated and worsted. Until he came to place it there, she could not reach him to destroy the thing.

She left her home without warning. The next day the Old

Woman had appeared, sitting all day on the stone sill. The *anwahs* followed as soon as the horrified leaders had discovered where their *mikuna* was, and that she would not return.

There were more conferences, each less fertile and less hopeful than the last. The climate, the weather, the material state of the planet grew every day more chaotic, more frightening. And still the Old Woman sat, and fought off the *anwahs,* and waited.

On a bright sunny morning in spring something suddenly pierced through her. She sprang to her feet, waving her invisible tormentors away.

A car had driven down Willy Street to the bank entrance and stopped. A man got out.

He had not moved two steps when an old woman confronted him. She did not touch him, she did not speak. She only looked at him and used her power.

He gasped, he clutched his throat, he fell to the sidewalk, and he lay there. He did not move again.

In the instant before the crowd gathered, the woman thrust her hand within his coat as if to feel his heart. Her handbag opened and shut. Then she was not there.

"Did anybody else see it?" asked the policeman after the doctor had pronounced him dead and the ambulance had taken him away.

"There was an old woman," said a voice. "She was leaning over him when I got there. But I don't see her now."

"Aw, don't bother about her—she's crazy," volunteered the retired bus dispatcher. "She's always here, but she can't even talk. Anyway she'll be back—all this commotion just scared her away."

"She don't matter," the white-bearded man in the ragged overcoat agreed. "She just sits here all day long, waving her arms around. Ought to've been put away long ago. I'm surprised she'd even walk up and look at him."

"We've done everything," said the Secretary of Defense wearily. "The whole FBI has been on the job day and night. There's no trace of it."

"But it *must* be found." The President's face was white. "His wife is absolutely certain he had it with him. You talked to him on the phone yourself."

"I know. We've gone all over that. I said to him, 'Do you mean there's only one copy of the formula in existence?' and he said, 'Except in my head,' and laughed. He was the greatest physicist alive, but you couldn't control him. You remember what a tussle we had to make him agree to give it to us alone instead of to the whole UN.

" 'You come right back to Washington with it then,' I told him, 'and let us put it where it will be safe. Suppose something happened to you?' I asked him. And he laughed again, and said, 'Nothing will. I'll bring it in when you're ready to start implementing it. Till then I want to be the only one who can lay hands on it.

" 'But I'll tell you what I'll do,' he said, 'if it will make you feel better. I'll put that copy in my safe-deposit box next time I'm in the city, and keep it there until you give me the word to come and get things started.' "

"But it isn't there," said the President. "My guess is that's what he was preparing to do when he dropped dead. It was a week later, but it would take him that long to get around to it. He must have had it on him somewhere. What was that story about an old woman who disappeared?"

"You know as much about it as I do. There was a crazy old woman used to be seen around there all the time. Somebody said she was leaning over him right after he fell. She hasn't been back and nobody knows where to find her. We had a house-to-house search of the whole city."

The President got up from his desk and began pacing the floor.

"And that's just it," he said in a strangled voice. "It's bad enough to think we've lost it. Didn't that damned fool of a genius know his heart was diseased? Nobody else is near the solution; he worked on it for sixteen years, and it may be centuries, or forever, before someone works it out again. But if that old woman was a foreign agent—"

"I keep hoping against hope that there was no connection," said the Secretary of Defense faintly. "I keep hoping that she *was* just some old lunatic who was frightened away by seeing him die. Then if we do find her we can get it back, and even if we don't, she'd never know what she had and, as you say, all we lose is the greatest scientific discovery in history.

"But there's always the other possibility, and we might as well face it. We've tightened the security program, but we can never be absolutely sure. If *they* have that formula, we might as well throw away all our atomic weapons and just wait to be annihilated."

"That's what it looks like. Even if we could put the whole population literally underground, it would be worse than useless."

"It would help *them*. From now on, we'll be living on the edge of a live crater."

"We've been doing that for years; there's no language to express the situation now." said the President.

"We'll keep on hunting, of course, but there's only one way out that I can see. We'll have to take a few key people in the UN, and in Congress too, into our confidence, and we'll have to do the biggest diplomatic job that ever was done on the earth.

"The way things stand now, it's peace—lasting peace—or the end of us all—eventually of them as well as us. *He* thought of it only in terms of the exploration of space—remember how he talked about those millions of suns and their planets to be conquered and colonized?

"But if another nation—and a nation that's our enemy—has the secret of counter-gravity—"

"Oh, God!" said the Minister of Defense, and his tone was reverent.

There was another of the endless conferences going on—each time they called it the last. But this one was more despairing than ever before—she had gone out of range. The *anwahs* had reverberated back. The range-finders were searching desperately, and all they could report was failure.

"Then this is really the end," groaned the leader of leaders; and all they could do was nod in unhappy agreement. "She has escaped us. We are doomed."

And then the ceiling door, where the sentries guarded their meeting, opened suddenly. And the Old Woman—who was no longer the Old Woman—stepped demurely to her vacant place.

She held up an imperative hand against their exclamations.

"Later, later," their *mikuna* said. "I've found something, and destroyed it, and at least postponed the very worst thing that could ever happen to us.

"And now," she added briskly, "What's all this about the weather?"

THE APOTHEOSIS OF KI

Ki became a mighty medicine man because he encountered a god and the god entered into him.

He was hunting alone; there were no longer enough young strong men in the tribe to hunt in groups. Every year the snow came farther south. Where his father had killed horses and bison still, there roamed the woolly mammoth and the reindeer. Of animals that one man can attack, few were left, and often the people were hard put to it to subsist on the grubs and eggs, the roots and berries and nuts, gathered by the women in the summer and put by. For more and more of the year, there was no living except in the caves, and a fire had to be kept going constantly outside, for comfort as well as for protection.

Ki found himself now crossing a wide plain he knew well. Once it had been a prized and precious hunting-ground; now he had searched for hours and found no living creature but himself. His heart was low within him, and in despair he glanced upward into the sky for help.

And then suddenly there was a noise like innumerable thunderbolts, and a flash like innumerable lightning-darts, so that he threw himself on the ground to hide his eyes. In the very midst of the plain something shaped like a giant egg had crashed to earth and burst into flames.

Dazed, Ki stood up and gaped at it. A crack in it opened and . . . somebody? something? crawled out and ran toward him, away from the blaze.

It was like a human being in shape, but vastly tall—taller even than the Terrible Men from the Sunrise before whom Ki's own people fled in fear. Instead of the fur or hide garments which men wear, he (it was male from its contours) was clad in some unknown material that was smooth and shiny, and around his head, resting on his shoulders, was a globular object that threw back glints from the winter sun, as if it were a giant misformed icicle. Then the being reached up and drew this from him, and his face was no human face, not even the weird unholy face of the Terrible Men. There were no ridges at all above the brow, but only a high pale dome; the chin, instead of retreating as does a man's, thrust outward; and the eyes, Ki saw, awed, were the color of river water.

Then Ki knew it was a god—though whether Akku of the Sky or Ber the Fire God or Hegag the God of Storms it was not given to mortal man to guess. Ki sank trembling to his knees, and the god walked nearer to him, and spoke. His voice was like the voice of wind in the trees, and Ki understood not a word he said. But Ki spoke also, if in no answer.

"O great god," he cried, "you have come! You have come as our fathers foretold to us, as our shaman promised us before he died and left us with no medicine man to mediate for us. You have come to help the tribe of Ki-ya, lest the young men die off beneath the cold, and the women and children starve in the caves, and the mighty and glorious people cease to be."

But the god stood and shook his strange head, and Ki understood then that the gods do not speak the language of men, any more than men can speak the language of the gods.

Yet still it seemed to him, as he knelt trembling in his worn furs that had been his father's and his father's father's, that in some manner beyond speech the god comprehended what he had said. For he raised an arm and pointed above him.

And Ki went on speaking to the god in his own tongue, which was the only tongue he knew.

"I see now that you are Akku of the Sky," he said. "Or if not Akku himself, then one from among his sons. I hear and obey, great god. Tell me now how we shall find sufficient food, so that we may live and grow strong again as once we were."

And as if he had known the meaning of the word *food*, the god opened his own mouth and pointed to it with his finger, and then pointed to his belly, where men feel hunger.

But gods do not eat and do not hunger, so Ki understood that it was he and his tribe whose need to eat was known to the god.

"True, but how?" Ki persisted. And the god gestured further. He swayed on his long legs like a man weak from fasting, and closed his eyes, and staggered as if he would fall.

And all the while the huge egg which had fallen from the sky and from which the god had emerged continued to blaze and crackle as if something more than wood fed it, though it is well known that only wood can burn.

"I am but a poor weak mortal," Ki pleaded desperately, "and the thoughts of the gods are too far beyond my thoughts. If it be your will, give me to understand how it is that our help is to come from you, and what I must do to carry out your commands."

Then with a stab of anguish it came to him that the god had meant by his pantomime that only by sacrifice would the tribe be saved, and that he desired Ki to lie down in the snow and die, as the god had feigned a man's doing.

Ki was a man full-grown; sixteen times the winter had come since he was a bawling infant at his mother's breast. But he was young still, and the juice and protest of youth were in him. Through his mind flashed thronging memories—memories of a child at play with his brothers, memories of the good years when the tribe had been strong and had feasted, memories of women he had had and of women he had wanted.

When men die, they sleep, the old medicine man had told them—all his class of boys gathered in the forest to be readied for their initiation. This was one of the mysteries that women and children must never hear. They sleep, and we lay them under the earth on a bed of branches, or in a dark inner corner of a cave, with flint flakes for their pillow. And around them we lay their weapons and tools, and the bones of the animals we have burnt and eaten in their honor, so that when at last they awaken—and only the gods can know when that will be—they may have near at hand weapons to defend themselves, and the reminders of sacrifice with which to uphold their dignity.

And Ki reflected that now the tribe had so fallen away that even the mightiest warriors and hunters died, and there were no animals to sacrifice to them. More still: when children died, or old women—great-grandmothers who had seen the changes of forty years or more—and even old men who left no descendants to fight for them, instead of being sacrificed to, they themselves became perforce their own sacrifice; and the tribe stilled its hunger by feeding on its own, so that only the bones were left to bury—and those blackened by fire and split to obtain the marrow and smeared with red earth so that when the dead awakened they might think the blood still ran through them. Worse: these two years past, only those who had been killed by beasts or by the Terrible Men from the Sunrise (for they no longer had warriors enough to raid other tribes of their own kind) still were taboo and must be buried as they fell.

That taboo had been ordained before the old medicine man felt himself close to death by some poison or ill-thinking—as death always comes that is not by direct killing. Ki remembered how one night around the fire the shaman had said, "This is the law which the people must obey even if they perish. For if even those killed by beasts or men were not taboo, then men would slay their own fellowmen of the tribe, only to feed on them." So he saw to it, when some evil-wisher from some other tribe had put weakness into his own body, that a young man of the tribe should strike him with his cudgel until he fell. It was done in full assembly before them all, that men might know it was by the shaman's own will, and the slayer be innocent.

It was Ki himself who had been chosen for that rite. It was the very cudgel he carried now, in sight of the god, with which he had done the deed.

All these things Ki remembered, and his heart did not wish to die. Least of all to die here, alone before the god. Who then of all the people would know of his sacrifice? Who would ever come to bury his body, and to know that it was worthy of honor?

But man is as nothing before the will of the gods, who rule breath and light and warmth and all that men must have, and rule also the wicked complaints and rebellions of the hearts of men.

So he rose and stood before the god and said, "If this be your will, I am ready. Slay me that the tribe may grow strong again."

But the god did not move to strike him. He had indeed in his hand, as Ki saw now, something, of some unknown divine shape and nature, too small for a cudgel and too large for a hand-ax, that might serve him as a weapon. But he did not raise it; instead he cast it from him, and let it lie where it fell in the snow, and he came nearer to Ki and held out his empty hands; and then once more he pointed to his mouth and to his belly. And he spoke again, in his tongue that no man could understand; and in his tone, had he been a man and not a god, was what would have seemed a note of pleading.

And Ki trembled, trying beyond his power of thought to comprehend.

And the god pointed again upward to the sky, and then to himself, and then, turning, to the sunrise and the sunset, and to the north and last to the south. And his voice was a question, asked with resignation but with the shadow of hope.

And so at last Ki understood.

With his cudgel he struck the god full on the head, and the god fell. And Ki struck him again and again until he lay still and his blood was on the snow.

Then he cast the dead god on the flames that still rose from the burning egg, and when the holy flesh was roasted he drew it forth, and when it was cool he hung it by a thong across his shoulders.

But first he ate the heart.

Before the sun was low in the sky, he reached the cave, and he threw his burden down before him as they came crowding out to see.

"Here is food," he said. "It is the body of a god, of a son of Akku of the Sky, who died that the people might live.

"And I have eaten his heart, and the god has entered into me and given me wisdom. Now I shall be your medicine man, and I shall guide you and teach you, and while you obey me I shall lead you to good hunting grounds, so that the people may wax fat again, and be many, as they once were, and be strong. And with tomorrow's sun, with the vigor that this meat will give us, we shall turn southward, for that is the last direction in which the god pointed.

"All this the god told me without words, before he commanded me to strike him dead. And if any doubt me, let him go to the plain beyond the dark forest, and he will find there what fire has left of a huge and monstrous egg, in which the god rode down from the sky, and appeared before me, Ki, to ransom and redeem the tribe of Ki-ya."

And two young men who did not believe went as he

commanded, and found that it was so. And they ate of the sacrifice, and at the next dawn they traveled southward.

Thus it was that Ki became a mighty medicine man. The god had entered into him, and he was as a god. And far to the south, where the snow and ice had not yet come, the tribe found good hunting, so that they grew strong again, and many children were born and did not die, and the tribe of Ki-ya raided and slew their enemies of many other tribes, and so became great once more upon the earth.

That all this is true is certain. For it was not until Ki had grown weak and very old—nearly fifty years still alive in the world—and his son's son, who envied him his wealth of flint and furs and women and meat and power, had cleft open his head with a stone ax and slain him, that the tribe of Ki-ya was overwhelmed and destroyed by a wandering horde of the Terrible Men from the Sunrise.

FREAK SHOW

"Who runs this outfit?" Rasi asked the first roustabout he saw on the carnival lot. He flicked a thumb toward the poster announcing the Human Oddities.

"Spencer," grunted the roustabout.

"Is he around?"

"Don't know why not."

Rasi lifted the flap of the tent, and found it empty. He walked toward the cluster of trailers drawn up on the new grounds an hour before. He had followed the carnival all night from its pitch of yesterday.

He knocked at the door of the nearest trailer. It opened a crack and a colorless eye in a pink face crowned by snow-white fluffy hair peered out at him. He had been lucky; this must be one of the Oddities.

"Can you tell me where I can find Mr. Spencer?"

A pink arm, apparently unclothed, pointed to the left.

"That's his car, over there—the green one with the window curtains," said a husky feminine voice. "But brother, watch your step. He's mad as hops. Goofoo the Nuthead didn't show up today. Blotto again, I wouldn't wonder. Prob'ly locked in the hoosegow at Cedartown."

Goofoo—so that was the name, the stage name at least, of the likely-looking one he'd picked up after the carnival closed last night in that other town. Three drinks from his special flask, and

Goofoo had been easy to deposit in a nearby cornfield to sleep it off for 24 hours or so. Everything was working out right.

Spencer came to the door with an irritated frown, but at least he was dressed. It was easier to look at them when they were covered. Rasi had been intensively trained and explicitly briefed, his camouflage was perfect, but nobody can control his psychological reactions completely.

"Mr. Spencer?" he said. "It's about a job. I was told there might be a vacancy."

The heavy-set middle-aged man with a shock of greying hair stared at him.

"Who told you?" he growled. "Anyway, I run a freak show. There'd be nothing for you."

"If I may come in for a moment—"

The manager opened the door grudgingly and stepped aside. It was a neat little place, shipshape and compact—a lot better, Rasi guessed, than the spot that would be allotted to him if he should be taken on.

Spencer sat down on the bunk and waved him to the chair.

"Make it snappy," he said. "I've bailed out that drunken idiot for the last time. But you couldn't take his place."

Rasi did not answer. Instead, he took off his hat, then his wig. Then slowly he removed the mask, with its unobservable transparency in the middle of the forehead. Spencer sat with his mouth open, his face turning slightly green. Rasi pulled off his gloves. He stooped and began to unfasten his shoes. Spencer put up his hand.

"That's enough." His voice sounded thick. "I don't know. I thought I'd seen everything. It might be too much—I don't want to have to be paying damages to women who have miscarriages after they see you.

"Good God, man, how have you got by up to now?"

"With the mask, and the wig, and shoes and gloves," said Rasi calmly. What would Spencer think, he reflected, if he knew that his own appearance was as revolting to his visitor as the visitor's could possibly be to him? And there were so many more of Spencer's kind!

"Then why do you— And why pick this outfit? If you can put it across at all, you could be a headliner with the Biggest Show on Earth."

"That's just what I don't want. I didn't choose to be like this. The fewer people I make sick the better. But I have to do something; I've come to the end of my money. So I have to use my only asset."

Spencer was recovering; the showman was taking over. He gazed meditatively at Rasi.

"If the costume was right—" he murmured. "And with a good spiel. You can't talk—that's it. You're a—I've got it! You're a Martian captured alive from a flying saucer that crashed. How would that do?"

Rasi repressed his amusement.

"Wouldn't your—wouldn't the government be interested in that? That Air Force project that's investigating?"

"They wouldn't bother. Just the fact that you're a carny attraction would prove to them that you're a phony. That whole flying saucer business is just bushwa, anyway. O.K.?"

"O.K."

"So let's talk money. You understand this isn't any million-dollar set-up, don't you? We can't pay much. And this is just a try-out."

"When you've got the job, somewhere in the Middle West of North America, report in," the Director had said. "Then we'll give you your detailed instructions about the later sowing."

"I feel like a beginner."

"I know what you mean. But a beginner wouldn't have got this assignment; we picked you from the whole Service. This is the big one, Rasi. Time's running short; we've got to get out of here. The ships won't last much longer. They were hardly fit to take off in after the Antea disaster. And you're perfect; you've got it all down, the language, the background, everything. With the mask, I defy any of them to guess."

"That's just it. If I'm to appear half of the time looking like a human being—"

"Like what *we* call a human being, Rasi: don't forget that. They call themselves human beings too, remember."

"Well, whatever. Isn't there danger I'll be recognized before I can get things set?"

"By whom? You must realize they're a lopsided lot. They've progressed mechanically, but they're primitives psychically and socially. And like all primitives, they're a mass of conceited arrogance. There's not one in a million of them that honestly believes, deep down, they aren't alone in the universe. To them, you'll be just a freak—especially when we've taken the precaution to keep you away from the most populous centers. That's why we picked this method."

"Am I permitted to ask if that is the only reason you chose that particular sector?"

"No, not the only one. The *buad* will radiate fastest from the center of a continent. And the middle of summer is the fastest-growing season."

"But then that will leave the whole Southern Hemisphere unaffected. Shouldn't there be two of us—one in each hemisphere?"

"We think not. It will spread in both directions. By the time their summer's over, it will be spring in the southern half and the *buad* will proliferate there."

"And when I've sowed all of it, you'll recall me? Excuse me for being insistent, Director, but I've got my sex-group and our offspring to consider."

"You'll be recalled—unless you get yourself killed first."

Rasi had expected to find it hard to associate with the rest of the freaks. But they differed so little from the normal population that his revulsion was lost in his general qualms. And they did not seem to shrink from him as he had anticipated—as the public shrank in horror. He found out why very soon.

Within a few days he had discovered that though such freaks as the Fat Lady (why was there never a Fat Gentleman?) or the Living Skeleton or the albino girl who first directed him to Spencer were formed by nature, and such as the Tattooed Man and the Fire Swallower were permanently modified by outside agencies, the Human Oddities included also downright fakes, like Roseanne.

Roseanne was the Headless Girl, with nothing above her very décolleté gown but a network of tubes and pipes. She was done with mirrors. She and the albino, whose name was Ethel, roomed together. The first night, when the last show was over, Roseanne strolled over to him.

"Hi!" she called. "Welcome to the madhouse. Where you sleeping?"

That had been his chief worry. He would take willingly the lowest pay that wouldn't arouse suspicion, but he must have a place of his own where he could have privacy. He needn't have bothered. He inherited the trailer which had accommodated Goofoo. Every man in the show had served notice at the beginning of the season that he was quitting if he had to bunk with Goofoo. The place was filthy, but he could clean it out. He told Roseanne where he was.

"We've got three days here," she said, "so there's no packing to do tonight. We thought, Ethel and me, maybe you'd like to come over to our joint for a nightcap. After you've got your disguise off, of course—Ethel's cat'd have her kittens too early if she got a sight of you the way you are!"

Then he understood: they took it for granted that the mask, in which Ethel had seen him that morning, was his real face. A weight of apprehension dropped from him.

"Natch!" he said. "Be there in ten minutes."

"Not that your get-up isn't a humdinger," Roseanne added. "It would fool smarter folks than these yokels. It almost scares *me.*"

"Too good for this crummy small-time carny, if you ask me," commented Ethel in her husky voice. Just being an albino wasn't enough of a show; she danced and sang torch songs too.

Before he left the trailer he activated the set implanted at the base of his brain and reported to the Director. Reception was pretty good.

He noted carefully in his memory-bank the instructions for distributing the *buad.*

A single grain of *buad* was enough. Each time the carnival left for a new pitch, Rasi deposited a grain in the lot. It should begin proliferating within a day. The effects would start a week later, long after he was miles away. It spread so fast in all directions that it was impossible to trace it to any particular focus.

The weeks went on. Rasi watched anxiously for news. By this time there should be rumors, at least. The carnival season would end in less than two months. Finally he could wait no longer: he put in an emergency call to the Director.

"You should not have called," said the Director sternly. "We had to risk one call to get you started, but we can't take a chance on having one of their astronomers get suspicious about unaccountable disturbances."

"I'm beginning to wonder—could the *buad* be too old?"

"It's all we have left, Rasi, after Antea. It was tested and passed. It's got to work.

"Are you having any other trouble?"

"Not to speak of—I'm having some difficulty keeping away from one of the female freaks, that's all."

Rasi could feel the vibrations of the Director's amusement.

"I won't tell your family. Just watch yourself."

"Oh, I am!"

But it wasn't so easy. Roseanne hung around all the time.

"I can't bear these real freaks," she told him. "I don't mean Ethel—she's O.K. The poor kid can't help being born without any pigment in her skin. But the men—ugh! After all, I don't belong in a joint like this. I've entertained in some swell night clubs. But I had a run of bad luck—"

And so on. All of which was gratifying, since it proved she didn't suspect him. But it kept him acting a part all the time.

He got nothing useful from his call to the Director. Either the *buad* would start working soon, or it was no good. Rasi turned cold; he knew what that would mean. If only Antea hadn't gone sour! Eight generations since their own home exploded, the few thousand survivors living and breeding in their ships and hunting desperately for a place where they could live, then locating Antea, and feeling that their troubles were over. A Preparer just like him had landed there, sowed the *buad,* waited till it softened up the inhabitants; and then they had taken over. Then barely a hundred years, with the ships slowly rusting in port, and the same thing all over again—a sun about to turn into a nova, a scramble for the ships, and out into space once more: but this time with ships that wouldn't last for another eight generations.

And now here was this perfect planet—and what was wrong with the *buad?* The fate of all of them depended on him alone; the Director didn't need to tell him that. Once, when he was very young and just starting training, he had asked why they needed the *buad*—why not just move in? Or why not ask to be allowed to colonize?—there weren't so many of them that they couldn't find an island nobody else wanted.

Because, he was told patiently, so far as they knew, there was no other race exactly like themselves—no other really human race, was the way they put it. And xenophobia seemed to be a disease as widespread as the galaxy. They couldn't conquer a planet by force, with their own ingrown pacifism—and there wouldn't be enough of them anyway. There was no hope that they would be welcomed as colonists by any alien race.

The answer was the *buad,* the wonderful plant that was all they had saved of value from their ruined far-off home. There, everyone had grown up under its influence, and the mutation had bred true. Nobody knew how long ago in the dim past the *buad's* strange properties had been discovered. Once sowed, the tiny, shining grains spread like wildfire, and as soon as the quick-growing plant was ripe its spores filled the air with an invisible, impalpable dust, harmless to breathe, but with a specific effect on the nervous system. No one who breathed *buad*-dust could ever be belligerent or aggressive or angry again: there could be no wars or fights or murders in a *buaa*-planted land. It had turned the fierce inhabitants of Antea in a few months into a friendly, receptive populace, and his people, freely welcomed, had settled there amicably. It would do the same for this planet—but not if the precious grains, so carefully preserved for so many centuries, were no longer viable.

Summer was passing. There were only a few weeks left before it would be too late. All day Rasi, in his proper person, cavorted and glowered and gestured as a captive Martian. (That was ironic: the planet they called Mars had long ago been visited and found unlivable.) When the last show was over he hurried to his trailer to put on the disguise. Not to mingle with the others would have made him too conspicuous. Fortunately he had become labeled as Roseanne's boy friend, and she saw to it that other women kept hands off. More fortunately, he managed to include Ethel in most of their meetings; his training had taught him the sex mores of these people, and he knew—so different from their own customs!—he would be safe from any embarrassing moments as long as there were three of them together.

And every time the carnival moved, before he left he planted the *buad.* He remembered the report of the Preparer on Antea: within a week of his first planting, he had begun to hear rumors of its effects. Intertribal conflicts had ceased, enemies embraced, violent crime dropped to zero, even predatory animals, though not so strongly influenced, had grown less ferocious; yet the

Anteans had lost none of their natural liveliness and enterprise, any more than his own people had done.

But there were no such rumors here. This race had a primitive sort of communication, by sight and sound, which reported all untoward developments; it remained silent as to this. Indeed—and Rasi's heart sank—in the very town where he had planted *buad* three weeks before, a conflict had broken out between a group of workers and their employers that ended in a pitched battle and the calling of professional soldiers to intervene. That, he knew, would have been totally impossible if the *buad* grain had been good. But there was nothing more he could do. There was still one faint hope: perhaps some of the grains were still alive, even if the rest were not, and even one successful planting would be enough. All he could do was to keep on until the dwindling supply was exhausted. Precious as it was, he took to planting two or three grains instead of one at a time.

On a night in what they called August, the carnival packed to move to its next pitch. Rasi, ready and waiting for his trailer to be hitched to a truck, stepped as usual into the blackest shadow he could find, the seed-pouch in his hand. He was at the edge of the lot, where a spreading tree cast a broad black shade. He walked to it softly, looking carefully around to make sure he was alone, and stooped to soften the earth beneath the tree.

There was a mere whisper of sound. He stood and listened—was it only the leaves moving in the wind? Across the lot were the lights and bustle of departure; they would get to him in a few minutes; he must hurry. He stooped again, scooped out a tiny hole, laid three grains of *buad* within it, and turned to go.

If his sight and hearing had been like theirs he would have missed it: he must indeed have missed it all the times before. Quicker than they could move, he reached down, and his hand caught a wrist and clamped on to it.

He pulled the struggling figure up and dragged the intruder away from the shadow.

It was Roseanne.

She tried to clench her fist, but he forced the fingers open so that the bits of dirt fell into his glove. Even in the darkness he could see the three shining grains of *buad.*

She stopped struggling and stood still.

"So you know," Rasi said quietly. "You know who I am and what I am doing here."

She gazed at him calmly.

"Not enough," she answered, and he noticed the different intonation from that of the raucous Roseanne he knew. "Not just who or just what—but enough to stop you."

He *could* not grow angry; he came of a race conditioned by breathing *buad*. But his voice shook.

"You have followed me every time," he accused her, "and undone my plantings."

"Every time."

"But why? Why, when you didn't even understand?"

"Because I knew from the beginning you were alien—you were not one of us. And I knew whatever you were doing here must be for your own ends, which are not ours."

"Listen," he said desperately, "we've been friends—"

"Have we?"

"I realize now you were only keeping me under surveillance. But let me explain."

"Go on."

"My people have no home. We could find one here, if you would let us come. This plant, this plant whose seeds you have dug up and thrown away—"

"Not thrown away: destroyed."

The last hope died, that she had scattered them where some might sprout. But he went on, heavily.

"They could do no harm. All they would do would be to spread a dust of spores that makes those who breathe it kind and gentle. Is that so bad?"

"Bad enough, when it means that then this planet would be softened to welcome an alien invasion."

"But what do you care?" he cried. "We wouldn't hurt you. All we want is a quiet spot where the few thousands there are left of us could live in peace."

"This is *our* planet," Roseanne said, and her voice was hard. "We got here first."

She laughed suddenly.

"Did you honestly think I was fooled by that mask and wig and all the rest? It was so easy to deceive a cheap carny entertainer, wasn't it? It never occurred to you that I was *waiting* for you to turn up—I here and others of us in half a hundred other likely places."

"You mean you intercepted our communications—even

between the ships? Who—who are you?"

She laughed again.

"Does it matter?" she mocked. "Who knows?—perhaps I'm from the CIA!"

So. Their own information had been faulty, after all—this race was far more developed than they had guessed. Developed so far as social mechanics went; psychologically they were just as primitive as he had expected. And now there would be no chance to change them by sowing the *buad.* His mission had failed. He and his people were doomed.

"Ready to roll, Rasi?"

It was Spencer's voice, from his car. Rasi looked around—the trucks and trailers were leaving the lot.

"We'll be along, Mr. Spencer," said Roseanne brightly. "See you tomorrow morning in Evartsville even if we have to take a bus to get there."

The manager smiled meanly at a private joke which Rasi understood. Whoever else was fooled, Spencer knew the Rasi on the platform of freaks was the real Rasi. If Roseanne hadn't found out yet—

"O. K., Roseanne, I can count on you," he chuckled. "Have a good time, kids. See you."

They could hear his sardonic laugh as he drove away. They were left alone on the deserted lot.

Rasi said nothing. He waited.

"I had no orders to turn you in," Roseanne said at last. "You know now it's no use your trying. We'll be here, watching. If I let you go, what will happen?"

"I'll be taken back to my ship. They'll send an autosub for me."

"What they—what we call a flying saucer?"

"I suppose so. One kind of them, anyway."

"And then what?"

"Then we'll go on searching, I suppose, till the ships or the *buad* give out. There's not much chance—and the *buad* grains are nearly all gone."

"You'll clear out of the skies here altogether?"

"Yes—there's nothing more in this system for us."

"Can you get word now to your ship? . . . Don't be foolish: we've intercepted you before."

He activated the transmitter to the Director's frequency.

Roseanne watched the autosub out of sight, till the last flicker of the revolving blue light was gone. Then, standing in the vacant carnival lot, she raised her wristwatch to her lips.

In another language, she said softly:

"Reporting. He's cleared out. The whole fleet should go very soon now; you can have them traced to make certain.

"That's the last. He was the only one of his kind, and we got rid of all the others. There are no invaders left.

"Except us, of course."

THE EEL

He was intimately and unfavorably known everywhere in the Galaxy, but with special virulence on eight planets in three different solar systems. He was eagerly sought on each; they all wanted to try him and punish him—in each case, by their own laws and customs. This had been going on for 26 terrestrial years, which means from minus ten to plus 280 in some of the others. The only place that didn't want him was Earth, his native planet, where he was too smart to operate—but, of course, the Galactic Police were looking for him there too, to deliver him to the authorities of the other planets in accordance with the Interplanetary Constitution.

For all of those years, The Eel (which was his Earth monicker; elsewhere, he was known by names indicating equally squirmy and slimy life-forms) had been gayly going his way, known under a dozen different aliases, turning up suddenly here, there, everywhere, committing his gigantic depredations, and disappearing as quickly and silently when his latest enterprise had succeeded. He specialized in enormous, unprecedented thefts. It was said that he despised stealing anything under the value of 100 million terrestrial units, and most of his thefts were much larger than that.

He had no recognizable *modus operandi,* changing his methods with each new crime. He never left a clue. But, in bravado, he signed his name to every job: his monicker flattered him, and after each malefaction the victim—usually a government agency, a giant corporation, or one of the clan enterprises of the smaller planets—would receive a message consisting merely of the impudent depiction of a large wriggling eel.

They got him at last, of course. The Galactic Police, like the prehistoric Royal Canadian Mounted, have the reputation of always catching their man. (Sometimes they don't catch him till he's dead, but they catch him.) It took them 26 years, and it was a hard job, for The Eel always worked alone and never talked afterward.

They did it by the herculean labor of investigating the source of the fortune of every inhabitant of Earth, since all that was known was that The Eel was a terrestrial. Every computer in the Federation worked overtime analyzing the data fed into it. It wasn't entirely a thankless task, for, as a by-product, a lot of embezzlers, tax evaders, and lesser robbers were turned up.

In the end, it narrowed down to one man who owned more than he could account for having. Even so, they almost lost him, for his takings were cached away under so many pseudonyms that it took several months just to establish that they all belonged to the same person. When that was settled, the police swooped. The Eel surrendered quietly; the one thing he had been surest of was never being apprehended, and he was so dumfounded he was unable to put up any resistance.

And then came the still greater question: which of the planets was to have him?

Xystil said it had the first right because his theft there had been the largest—a sum so huge, it could be expressed only by an algebraic index. Artha's argument was that his first recorded crime had been on that planet. Medoris wanted him because its only penalty for any felony is an immediate and rather horrible death, and that would guarantee getting rid of The Eel forever.

Ceres put in a claim on the ground that it was the only planet or moon in the Sol System in which he had operated, and since he was a terrestrial, it was a matter for local jurisdiction. Eb pleaded that it was the newest and poorest member of the Galactic Federation, and should have been protected in its inexperience against his thievishness.

Ha-Almirath argued that it had earned his custody because it was its Chief Ruler who had suggested to the police the method which had resulted in his arrest. Vavinour countered that it should be the chosen recipient, since the theft there had included desecration of the High Temple.

Little Agsk, which was only a probationary Galactic Associate, modestly said that if it were given The Eel, its prompt and exemplary punishment might qualify it for full membership, and it would be grateful for the chance.

A special meeting of the Galactic Council had to be called for the sole purpose of deciding who got The Eel.

Representatives of all the claimant planets made their representations. Each told in eloquent detail why his planet and his alone was entitled to custody of the arch-criminal, and what they would do to him when—not if—they got him. After they had all been heard, the councilors went into executive session, with press and public barred. An indiscreet councilor (it was O-Al of Phlagon of Altair, if you want to know) leaked later some of the rather indecorous proceedings.

The Earth councilor, he reported, had been granted a voice but no vote, since Earth was not an interested party as to the crime, but only as to the criminal. Every possible system of arbitration had been discussed—chronological, numerical in respect to the size of the theft, legalistic in respect to whether the culprit would be available to hand on to another victim when the first had got through punishing him.

In the welter of claims and counterclaims, one harassed councilor wearily suggested a lottery. Another in desperation recommended handing The Eel a list of prospective punishments on each of the eight planets and observing which one seemed to inspire him with most dread—which would then be the one selected. One even proposed poisoning him and announcing his sudden collapse and death.

The sessions went on day and night; the exhausted councilors separated for brief periods of sleep, then went at it again. A hung jury was unthinkable; something had to be decided. The news outlets of the entire Galaxy were beginning to issue sarcastic editorials about procrastination and coddling criminals, with hints about bribery and corruption, and remarks that perhaps what was needed was a few impeachments and a new general election.

So at last, in utter despair, they awarded The Eel to Agsk, as a sort of bonus and incentive. Whichever planet they named, the other seven were going to scream to high heaven, and Agsk was least likely to be able to retaliate against any expressions of indignation.

Agskians, as everyone knows, are fairly humanoid beings, primitives from the outer edge of the Galaxy. They were like college freshmen invited to a senior fraternity. This was their Big Chance to Make Good.

The Eel, taciturn as ever, was delivered to a delegation of six of them sent to meet him in one of their lumbering spaceships, a low countergrav machine such as Earth had outgrown several millennia before. They were so afraid of losing him that they put a metal belt around him with six chains attached to it, and fastened all six of themselves to him. Once on Agsk, he was placed in a specially made stone pit, surrounded by guards, and fed through the only opening.

In preparation for the influx of visitors to the trial, an anticipated greater assembly of off-planeters than little Agsk had ever seen, they evacuated their capital city temporarily, resettling all its citizens except those needed to serve and care for the guests, and remodeled the biggest houses for the accommodation of those who had peculiar space, shape, or other requirements.

Never since the Galactic Federation was founded had so many beings, human, humanoid, semi-humanoid and non-humanoid, gathered at the same time on any one member planet. Every newstape, tridimens, audio, and all other varieties of information services—even including the drum amplifiers of Medoris and the ray-variants of Eb—applied for and were granted a place in the courtroom. This, because no other edifice was large enough, was an immense stone amphitheater usually devoted to rather curious games with animals; since it rains on Agsk only for two specified hours on every one of their days, no roof was needed. At every seat, there was a translatophone, with interpreters ready in plastic cages to translate the Intergalactic in which the trial was conducted into even the clicks and hisses of Jorg and the eye-flashes of Omonro.

And in the midst of all this, the cause and purpose of it all, sat the legendary Eel.

Seen at last, he was hardly an impressive figure. Time had been going on and The Eel was in his fifties, bald and a trifle paunchy. He was completely ordinary in appearance, a circumstance which had, of course, enabled him to pass unobserved on so many planets; he looked like a salesman or a minor official, and had indeed been so taken by the unnoticing inhabitants of innumerable planets.

People had wondered, when word came of some new outrage by this master-thief, if perhaps he had disguised himself as a resident of the scene of each fresh crime, but now it was obvious that this had not been necessary. He had been too clever to pick any planet where visitors from Earth were not a common sight, and he had been too insignificant for anyone to pay attention to him.

The criminal code of Agsk is unique in the Galaxy, though there are rumors of something similar among a legendary extinct tribe on Earth called the Guanches. The high priest is also the chief executive (as well as the minister of education and head of the medical faculty), and he rules jointly with a priestess who also officiates as chief judge.

The Agskians have some strange ideas to a terrestrial eye—for example, suicide is an honor, and anyone of insufficient rank who commits it condemns his immediate family to punishment for his presumption. They are great family people, in general. Also, they never lie, and find it hard to realize that other beings do.

Murder, to them, is merely a matter for negotiation between the murderer and the relatives of the victim, provided it is open and without deceit. But grand larceny, since property is the foundation of the family, is punished in a way that shows that the Agskians, though technologically primitive, are psychologically very advanced.

They reason that death, because it comes inevitably to all, is the least of misfortunes. Lasting grief, remorse and guilt are the greatest. So they let the thief live and do not even imprison him.

Instead, they find out who it is that the criminal most loves. If they do not know who it is, they merely ask him, and since Agskians never lie, he always tells them. Then they seize that person, and kill him or her, slowly and painfully, before the thief's eyes.

And the agreement had been that The Eel was to be tried and

punished by the laws and customs of the planet to which he was awarded.

The actual trial and conviction of The Eel were almost perfunctory. Without needing to resort to torture, his jailers had been presented, on a platter as it were, with a full confession—so far as the particular robbery he had committed on Agsk was concerned. There is a provision for defense in the Agskian code, but it was unneeded because The Eel had pleaded guilty.

But he knew very well he would not be executed by the Agskians; he would instead be set free (presumably with a broken heart) to be handed over to the next claimant—and that, the Council had decided, would be Medoris. Since Medoris always kills its criminals, that would end the whole controversy.

So the Eel was quite aware that his conviction by Agsk would be only the preliminary to an exquisitely painful and lingering demise at the two-clawed hands of the Medorans. His business was somehow to get out from under.

Naturally, the resources of the Galactic Police had been at the full disposal of the officials of Agsk.

The files had been opened, and the Agskians had before them The Eel's history back to the day of his birth. He himself had been questioned, encephalographed, hypnotized, dormitized, injected, psychographed, subjected to all the means of eliciting information devised by all eight planets—for the other seven, once their first resentment was over, had reconciled themselves and cooperated wholeheartedly with Agsk.

Medoris especially had been of the greatest help. The Medorans could hardly wait.

In the spate of news of the trial that inundated every portion of the Galaxy, there began to be discovered a note of sympathy for this one little creature arrayed against the mightiest powers of the Galaxy. Poor people who wished they had his nerve, and romantic people who dreamed of adventures they would never dare perform, began to say that The Eel wasn't so bad, after all; he became a symbol of the rebellious individual thumbing his nose at entrenched authority. Students of Earth prehistory will recognize such symbols in the mythical Robin Hood and Al Capone.

These were the people who were glad to put up when bets began to be made. At first the odds were ten to one against The Eel; then, as time dragged by, they dropped until it was even money.

Agsk itself began to be worried. It was one thing to make a big, expensive splurge to impress the Galaxy and to hasten its acceptance into full membership in the Federation, but nobody had expected the show to last more than a few days. If it kept on much longer, Agsk would be bankrupt.

For the trial had foundered on one insoluble problem: the only way The Eel could ever be punished by their laws was to kill the person he most loved—and nobody could discover that he had ever loved anybody.

His mother? His father? He had been an undutiful and unaffectionate son, and his parents were long since dead in any case. He had never had a brother, a sister, a wife or a child. No probing could find any woman with whom he had ever been in love. He had never had an intimate friend.

He did nothing to help, naturally. He simply sat in his chains and smiled and waited. He was perfectly willing to be escorted from the court every evening, relieved of his fetters and placed in his pit. It was a much pleasanter existence than being executed inch by inch by the Medorans. For all he cared, the Agskians could go on spending their planetary income until he finally died of old age.

The priestess-judge and her coadjutors wore themselves out in discussions far into the night. They lost up to 15 pounds apiece, which on Agsk, where the average weight of adults is about 40, was serious. It began to look as if The Eel's judges would predecease him.

Whom did The Eel love? They went into minutiae and subterfuges. He had never had a pet to which he was devoted. He had never even loved a house which could be razed. He could not be said to have loved the immense fortune he had stolen, for he had concealed his wealth and used little of it, and in any event it had all been confiscated and, so far as possible, restored proportionately to those he had robbed.

What he had loved most, doubtless, was his prowess in stealing unimaginable sums and getting away with it—but there is no way of "killing" a criminal technique.

Almost a year had passed. Agsk was beginning to wish The Eel had never been caught, or that they had never been awarded the glory of trying him.

At last the priestess-judge, in utter despair, took off her judge's robes, put on the cassock and surplice of her sacred calling, and laid the problem before the most unapproachable and august of the gods of Agsk.

The trial was suspended while she lay for three days in a trance on the high altar. She emerged weak and tottering, her skin light blue instead of its healthy purple, but her head high and her mouth curved in triumph.

At sight of her, renewed excitement surged through the audience. News-gatherers, who had been finding it difficult of late to get anything to report, rushed to their instruments.

"Remove the defendant's chains and set him free," the priestess-judge ordered in ringing tones. "The Great God of the Unspeakable Name has revealed to me whom the defendant most loves. As soon as he is freed, seize him and slay him. For the only being he loves is—himself."

There was an instant's silence, and then a roar. The Medorans howled in frustration.

But The Eel, still guarded but unchained, stood up and laughed aloud.

"Your Great God is a fool!" he said blasphemously. "I deny that I love myself. I care nothing for myself at all."

The priestess-judge sighed. "Since this is your sworn denial, it must be true," she said. "So then we cannot kill you. Instead, we grant that you do indeed love no one. Therefore you are a creature so far outside our comprehension that you cannot come under our laws, no matter how you have broken them. We shall notify the Federation that we abandon our jurisdiction and hand you over to our sister-planet which is next in line to judge you."

Then all the viewers on tridimens on countless planets saw something that nobody had ever thought to see—The Eel's armor of self-confidence cracked and terror poured through the gap.

He dropped to his knees and cried: "Wait! Wait! I confess that I blasphemed your god, but without realizing that I did!"

"You mean," pressed the priestess-judge, "you acknowledge that you yourself are the only being dear to you?"

"No, not that, either. Until now, I have never known love. But now it has come upon me like a nova and I must speak the truth." He paused, still on his knees, and looked piteously at the priestess-judge. "Are—are you bound by your law to—to believe me and to kill, instead of me, this—this being I adore?"

"We are so bound," she stated.

"Then," said The Eel, smiling and confident again, rising to his feet, "before all the Galaxy, I must declare the object of my sudden but everlasting passion. Great lady, it is you!"

The Eel is still in his pit, which has been made most comfortable by his sympathizers, while the Council of the Galactic Federation seeks feverishly and vainly, year after year, to find some legal way out of the impasse.

FIRST DIG

The day before the funeral, the family, what was left of it, had gathered in New Place—all but old Anne; feeble now, she was sleeping in the second-best bed he had left her. Susanna was there, and her husband Hall the physician, and their little daughter. Judith had brought her new husband Thomas Quiney, and the others were not pleased, as her father had not been. His sister, the newly widowed Mrs. Hart, was there with her three sons. She it was who had protested against the inscription on the tombstone.

"People will say he himself wrote it," she complained, "and it is a poor awkward thing."

"Nay, aunt," Susanna told her. "It must be as he asked. He is not to be buried in the churchyard with our grandparents, but in the church itself, before the altar, within the chancel rail. He has the right, as part owner of the village tithes. But we know well that would not protect him—nor the memory of the glory he has brought to this town, either—when the time came for some other tithe-owner to claim the honor of burial in that place. Then they would shovel his poor bones out into the charnel-house in the churchyard. He dreaded that, and it is for that reason that he commanded those words to be carved on the flagstone above his grave."

And so he was laid in his wooden coffin in the ground, with no vault, beneath the stone with its inscription; and none dared disobey the exhortation on it. And the years passed, and the centuries, and the millennia, and still he lay undisturbed . . . .

During the long vacation, whenever the planetary opposition was favorable, the archaeological department of the Central University took a group of students to the Old Planet for a two-week course in the technique of practical excavation. After 50,000 years the air was safe and breathable, though with a quality tense and bitter to the young people accustomed to the mechanically cleaned and warmed air of their home planets. But the field expeditions were popular, and there was always a waiting list.

This time Roland was the youngest of the group; others had made the trip before, but this would be his first dig. He was excited, full of romantic imaginings. The briefing session as soon as they landed was meant to take the nonsense out of young dreamers, but it did not succeed with Roland.

"Naturally," said Kan, the teaching assistant who was in charge, "you understand that the sites allocated to students are not those where important finds may be expected. The whole desert planet is in a sense one huge archaeological site, and of course anyone might find anything anywhere. But what you must expect is something quite humble—a kitchen midden, a heap of barren rubble that once was a minor public building, an insignificant village. This time we are to dig in what was apparently, for our remote ancestors in prehistory, a rural district far removed from such civilized centers as the inhabitants possessed."

"Just where on the Old Planet are we?" a student of palaeogeography wanted to know.

"I can tell you the longitude and latitude, but we have given no names to the various locations, and of course we have no idea what the people who lived in them called them. All I can say is that when there were oceans here, this must have been an island. Our exact position on the planet doesn't matter, except that it is far away from the poles, which seem always to have been uninhabited. What we're here for, as you know, is to learn the methods by which scientific digging is done. You'll have far more use for picks and knives and brushes and your own fingers than for any theoretical knowledge; that will come later, when we start classifying our finds—if we make any."

But even such dry injunctions were unable to discourage Roland. He received his allotment of space—some four by eight feet in a dreary waste of tumbled stone—with shining eyes, as if in his heart he knew something wonderful and thrilling must be waiting for him, and for him alone, beneath the blasted crust.

At the end of a hard day's labor with no appreciable results whatever—for of course no solvents or explosives could be used in this slow, patient, careful, primitive procedure—he alone still felt fresh enthusiasm. Kan watched him with a quizzical smile. But the smile was hopeful too; he had had his eye on Roland from the beginning. Perhaps once or twice in his career, a teacher discovers among cheerful mediocrities a born and dedicated scholar. Kan had faith that young Roland, once he had shed his juvenile thrill-seeking, had the makings of such a one.

It was only on the third day that one of the more experienced students made the first find—part of a human jaw. Others followed fast, until it became evident that they were in luck—the site, chosen for them at random, must once have been in part a cemetery, in part the ruins of an adjacent and perhaps related building. But Kan disparaged the finds.

"Nothing worth keeping," he ruled. "We have any amount of remains of this type already. We'll leave them here when we go."

So it was rather timidly, though exultantly, that Roland called to him late that afternoon.

"L-look," he stammered in his excitement. "There were no bones here—if there ever were any they must have coalesced long ago with the earth. But under the rubble I found this—it was broken across the middle but the crack fits perfectly."

At the side of the open excavation he had laid the stone slab, the two pieces carefully fitted together.

"It's simply covered with markings, Kan!"

"So I see." The teacher hesitated. Would it be wise to snub the boy too much? Still, it would do him no good to give him false ideas which he might find it hard to overcome.

"That's far from unique, you know, Roland," he said gently. "Our museums are running over with inscribed stone and metal. We know that most of the inhabitants of the Old Planet did have a written language—or many languages, for all that we can tell. But the trouble is, they are all entirely indecipherable, and probably always will be."

Roland looked at him aghast.

"Do you mean, with all our advanced technology, we can't read what they wrote?"

"I'm afraid not. You see, we have no clue whatever. If we had somewhere an inscription in parallel languages, and knew one of them, of course we could read the other. Or if we had even some inscription we could relate to known facts—a map, an astronomical chart—we might manage. But unfortunately they seem never to have inscribed such things on metal or stone, and their more perishable materials, whatever they were, have long since crumbled into dust. If the whole planet hadn't been blasted, some such things might have been preserved in dry caves or under deserts, even after 50,000 years. . . . No matter how advanced our own science, Roland, it is impossible to decipher an unknown language written in an unknown script, especially when we haven't even proper names to go by."

Kan glanced at the boy's downcast face, and added hastily: "But if you want to keep this as a souvenir of your first dig, I don't think there would be any objection. We've allowed weight for any posible finds of value."

Roland said slowly: "This—this must have been a marker on a grave. Wouldn't it have some important significance? Perhaps it would tell us about their religion."

"We don't even know if they had one. This could simply be a statement of the name and dates of the person buried here. We have thousands and thousands of similar gravestones in our museums. And is it likely that this one, from a rural district in an isolated corner of the planet, would be of the slightest importance?"

"But I had such a strong feeling—"

The teacher gazed at him keenly.

"Have you extra-sensory perception, Roland?" he asked.

"No, I haven't—at least that's what they said when I was examined in lower school. But my mother had, and sometimes I've felt I must have inherited just a little of it. I have such strong premonitions sometimes. Before I even touched this digging I felt there was a—a message here for me.

"And when I started to handle those broken pieces of stone—You'll think I'm crazy. But I felt I'd committed a crime—I felt guilty—

"It's as if I had disobeyed something—somebody from that remote past—some mighty spirit that will never die; as if I had disobeyed him and now I must be punished for it."

Kan stared at the boy in perplexity, wondering how to deal with him. Some of the others had stopped work and gathered around him, curious to see what was happening. "Has Roland found something valuable?" asked the girl who had been digging nearest to them.

"Nothing at all—we're talking about something else altogether," the teacher said brusquely. He dismissed them with a wave of the hand, and they turned back reluctantly to their own work. Roland was pale and trembling, his expression a mixture of shame and determination.

"I suppose you think I'm out of my mind," he said defensively to his teacher.

"No, I don't," Kan answered quietly. "Whether you are wrong or right in your feeling doesn't matter. What matters is that you should feel right within yourself. Perhaps you weren't meant to be an archaeologist, after all."

"Oh, but I am! Nothing has ever meant so much to me. It's just—this single find—"

"Put the stone back where you found it, Roland. I'll find another place for you to dig."

The boy began to shake uncontrollably.

"It's too late," he muttered. "I've committed the sin already."

"Put that stone back, and come away."

As if he had not heard, Roland reached into his kit and brought out a rolled piece of plastic and a marking-pen. He crouched on the ground beside the broken flagstone.

"I must copy the inscription first," he whispered. "I *must.*"

Kan put out a hand to stop him, then withdrew it halfway. Let him work out the compulsion. Perhaps it would act as a catharsis. Later, when Roland was calm again, they would talk about it and the teacher might find some way to avoid the destruction of so promising a career.

Unable to tear himself away, he stood watching Roland as laboriously he copied the senseless markings.

With the last letter, Roland looked up at him.

"It's finished," he said hoarsely, and thrust it into Kan's hand. "Keep it." The look in his eyes made Kan shudder.

"Oh, no!" Roland cried sharply. "I didn't mean to—"

Suddenly he slumped face downward on the open grave. Kan bent quietly and felt for his heart. It had stopped beating.

When the expedition returned, before its time because of the unexpected tragedy, an official inquiry determined that Roland's heart had not been equal to the over-exertion of digging. The University authorities were reprimanded for carelessness in certifying him as physically fit. Kan was absolved of all blame for his death.

But he blames himself bitterly. He kept the sheet of plastic with him, though neither he nor anyone else would ever know what those strange words meant. He could never bring himself to destroy it, or to show it to any other person. Sometimes he stared at it for long ruminative sessions, as if willing himself to force its secret from it, but in vain. He grew so familiar with it that he knew by heart the shape of every marking.

Roland had died because he believed that human genius has everlasting power, even when the name of the man who possessed it and that of the very land which gave him birth have both been obliterated from the memory of mankind—that some supreme genius of the prehistoric past had reached out through 50 millennia to strike down the vandal who had desecrated his last resting-place. He had believed those crooked marks had conveyed the warning.

In soberer moments Kan told himself not to be a fool. The boy, despite his talent, had been a complete neurotic; he had died of his neurosis and the physical exhaustion it had induced. To share in an atavistic yielding to such gross superstition was unworthy of the scientific position he himself, with the years and hard work, had attained.

But all his life that inscription haunted him. Sometimes at night when he could not sleep he could see it in his mind's eye before him, with all its maddening mystery:

GOOD FREND FOR JESVS SAKE FORBEARE,
TO DIGG THE DVST ENCLOASED HEARE;
BLESTE BE Y MAN Y SPARES THES STONES,
AND CVRST BE HE Y MOVES MY BONES.

Note: The above is a tracing of the actual inscription on Shakespeare's grave.

PRISON BREAK

Warden Miles Morgan looked at the five men he had summoned to his office. He could trust them all. They might well all die, and he with them, but while they lived no prisoner would escape.

Being a prison warden in the United States of America in 2033 was in one way a sinecure and in another way a responsibility almost too great for one fallible man. The Bates-Watson Law, passed in 2014 and finally declared constitutional by the Supreme Court in 2017—the court had ruled, 7 to 2, that it did not involve cruel and unusual punishment—had largely emptied the prisons, so far as new inmates were concerned. (The old ones were kept in special institutions until their terms expired.) For one thing, juries were reluctant to convict except on unimpeachable evidence; for another, the abandonment at last of the outmoded McNaghten Rule, and the requirement of unbiased psychiatric examination of each indicted person, had shifted from prisons to mental hospitals the huge number of borderline psychotics and psychopaths who once had made up the majority of the prison population; for still another, the new form of sentence acted as a genuine deterrent, as capital punishment never had done. A man hesitated a long time before committing a felony, when the chances were, not that he would serve five or ten years in a modern, enlightened prison and then come out to the world he had known, but that when his sentence was served (and parole was no longer possible) he would emerge as a stranger, with all his contemporaries physically five or ten years his seniors.

The Lingelbach-Yamasuto discovery of induced coma had made the Bates-Watson Law possible. Certain crucial neurons of the brain, the Swiss and Japanese scientists working together had proved, could be deactivated so long as the subject was kept at a temperature just above freezing-point. It was not entirely a new idea—as long ago as 1958 a science fiction writer named Clarke, in one of the startling extrapolations which so many science fiction authors of that time displayed, had suggested some such possibility, and even its application to penology. What was new was the means of achieving it, without permanent injury, and of ending it whenever the subject's term was up.

In consequence, one institution sufficed for each state—in fact, in some of the less crowded states, two or three used a common center. The former Federal penitentiaries, now that state and Federal penal institutions were one, were sometimes utilized. No provision need be made any more for feeding, clothing, employing, educating, entertaining, or disciplining mobile prisoners; the staffs consisted entirely of technicians and maintenance men, and one building which might have housed 1000 convicts could now easily accommodate several times that number, since they lay in long rows, aisle upon aisle, with the minimum nourishment given them by injection and their cleansing and massage (to avoid bedsores and stiffened limbs) easily handled by a few orderlies.

So when Miles Morgan became warden of San Quentin in 2028, he became the chief in command of all convicted felons in California. He was a big, rawboned man, young-looking still in 2033 at 52, with a steel-trap mind sharpened by years of intensive education and practical experience. For five years his charge had gone as smoothly as clockwork; he was an excellent administrator, and had no other duties in the ordinary course of things. What he was paid his large salary for—the reason he had been the unanimous choice of the Board of Prison Commissioners and the governor, the reason they had refused his proffered resignation at the end of his first year—was that in the face of an emergency he could be depended on to cope. A widower, his whole life was in the prison. He seldom left it, and he had closed the warden's residence after his wife's death and lived in a small bachelor apartment in the main building itself—a suite of rooms directly connecting with his large office.

He was there as usual on the morning of March 18, 2033, dictating to his civilian secretary, a good-looking thirtyish blonde named Mavis Brock, who had, however, been selected for her job not for her good looks but for her competence. Morgan's marriage had been a singularly happy one, and when it had ended with his wife's sudden death he had shut his emotions into a private cell that not even his few close friends ever dared to penetrate. He was far from cold, he was amiable and sociable, but something had broken in him when Laura died, and it had never been mended.

"Take a letter to Brown and Stacey," he was saying now to Miss Brock. "What has happened to the consignment of termite-proofing solution ordered by this office on February 10? We are in need of this material and must have it by the end of this week at the latest. If—"

At which instant all the papers slid off his desk, he and the secretary were both thrown to the floor in a tangled heap, and the entire stone building swayed sickeningly for many seconds and then came to a quivering stop.

An earthquake, of 7.2 intensity on the Richter scale, had opened up again the old San Andreas fault that runs from Point Arena to the Mojave.

The warden picked himself and Miss Brock up. It was characteristic of him that his first thought was for her, his second for the prison, and that, outside of a cursory examination to be sure he had no injuries, he gave none at all to himself.

"Better get home right away, Miss Brock, if you can," he said. "You'll be safer in your car than in a building, and your family will be worried about you."

"But can't I be of any help?" she asked. She commuted from near-by San Rafael.

"Not a bit; I'll take care of things here. Off you go. Watch out for fallen wires. Phone me how you find things at home."

He turned to the visiphone, to find out about damage. Before he could lift the receiver, Harry Monghetti, the head engineer, burst into the office without knocking. His face was white.

"You O.K., warden? Good. Look—something's happened."

"Bad damage?"

"Not to the building. But the shock broke the main freezer pipe."

"The emergency feeder working?"

"I checked right away. It will handle everything—except Ward H."

Ward H. They both knew what that meant. The long-termers, 20 to 50 years (nobody got life any more). The toughest and worst. And No. 30718, who had been there four years and had 46 still to go.

The warden snapped into action.

"Get the ward blocked off at once," he ordered. "The unfreezing doesn't take long. There are 82 men in that ward, and I want them kept there till we can secure enough force to subdue and refreeze them."

He turned to the phone as Monghetti ran from the room, and got the chief orderly at once.

"Larson? Have your men check all wards except H immediately. Tell Mrs. Carpentier to see to it that the women's ward is sealed off. Then come here for further orders."

The intercom was working all right. Now for the outside lines.

He reviewed the situation briefly. Staff. He had 63 men and women in all. None of them was a rough or a plug-ugly—those days were over in prison. All the tough subjects were on cots in neuron-freeze—or, in Ward H, coming out of it. Arms? Nothing, so far as he knew, but one cool-gun reposing in his own desk drawer. Blocking off Ward H wouldn't protect them very long. One of the 82 was a man named Farmer, a peterman who in a long and nefarious career, before he was caught at last, had built up a formidable reputation for opening, with the crudest instruments if necessary (say a wire off a cot-spring) any lock that the ingenuity of man had ever devised. Morgan must get effective help at once.

The State Police were going to be plenty busy handling the consequences of a major earthquake shock. He would have to have top priority to get any help out of them. He dialed the number of the governor's private line in Sacramento.

It rang twice before the first after-shock came. That wasn't so intense as the first one had been—things rocked and waved, but nothing fell, and Morgan stayed in his chair by hooking a foot around one of its legs.

But it was enough. The visiphone went dead.

Rapidly the warden went over in his mind the available help. Monghetti, Larson, a big orderly named Groutschmidt who used to be a welterweight prizefighter, another named Smith who knew judo, a technician named Salisbury whose hobby was plane-racing. The rest were indoor, studious types, useless, or worse, in this crisis. They could be of most service by getting out and spreading the word. Mrs. Carpentier and her three assistants must go immediately. As soon as they left, and the rest of the surplus staff members, the juice must be turned on in the outside gates and walls.

There just wasn't time for further detailed planning, Morgan thought as he lifted the receiver and ordered the chosen five to come to his office, and had the loudspeaker activated to get the rest of the staff out. This was the emergency that justified the sinecure. Outside aid might or might not arrive in time. Meanwhile, it was going to be six of them against 82. And he knew who the leader of the 82 would be, as soon as the men were unfrozen and had marshaled their forces: 30718. The warden shut his mind hard on that thought.

The five dependables came running. "Ward H blocked off," Monghetti reported. Everything else had been attended to, without argument. In the sense in which a ship with a good captain is a happy ship, San Quentin was a happy prison. His staff respected him and trusted him. More, they liked him: proof of that was that every one of them knew his tragedy and not one word of it ever passed their lips.

"I don't have to draw a picture for you," he told them when they had all assembled in his big office. "How long do you figure it will take, Harry," he asked Monghetti, "before they'll be outside the ward?"

"I'd say we have from 20 minutes to half an hour."

"Good. That gives us a breathing-space. Now let's put ourselves in their minds. The unfreezing will be quick and automatic—quite unlike the freezing process. They'll be a little weak for a few minutes, but not long—we've kept them in fine condition. Farmer will get them out of there in short order.

"Their first idea, of course, will be escape. We'll see them from the windows here—lucky for us they're shatterproof and one-way transparent. They'll find out that the walls and gates have been activated. Then what will they do?"

"They know the activation cut-off is here—or they'll guess it when they can't find it anywhere else. So they'll mass and attack us," Larson said.

"Wait a minute," Salisbury interposed. "Mayn't they try first to unfreeze the fellows in the other wards?"

"Not out of sympathy, that's for sure," said the warden. "And there's enough of them already—they won't need auxiliaries. Anyway, if they had any such notion, it wouldn't hold them up long; they'd discover very soon that they didn't know how. There are no technicians among them."

"Farmer could get them into the women's ward," Larson suggested.

"He could. But they won't waste their time that way, either. They'll want out, where there are plenty of women who aren't frozen zombies." Morgan drew a long breath. "They've got a brain among them, you know," he added quietly. "He'll think of things like that."

"Yeah—30718," Smith muttered. Nobody else said anything.

"So," the warden went on briskly, "in, say, half to three quarters of an hour this office is going to be turned into a fortress. Some of you may wonder why we don't just go up to Ward H and subdue them before they get going. Because we couldn't, that's why. They'd be on us and overpower us before we'd get well started, and we can't refreeze them anyway, with the pipe broken.

"We can't communicate with the outside, the quake fixed that; but there are 57 of our staff members—58 counting Miss Brock, if she got home safely—who are out already, and most of them realize the general situation. They'll see to their homes and families first, of course; that's to be expected. But then, barring another big temblor, they'll begin to pick up the threads. If the damage in this area hasn't been a lot worse than it was right here, and if all we get now is lessening after-shocks, it won't be very long before people are alerted. We'll get state police, police and firemen from San Rafael and the other Marin County towns, maybe even state guardsmen, or Federal troops from Hamilton Field or all the way from San Francisco. Hell, maybe just civilians with a sense of civic duty. They'll lift the siege for us. If we see them coming we can deactivate the gates."

"That's a lot of ifs," Groutschmidt growled. "It may take hours. Or days."

"Exactly," replied the warden calmly. "So it's up to us, till help comes, to hold the fort. We may all be killed. But until we are, nobody can reach the atomic activator that controls the walls and gates. We're the last redoubt. It's too late to let any of you out now, but if anybody would rather, there's time yet to lock himself in somewhere else where it might be safer."

"Nobody's going," said Larson.

"I didn't mean—" Groutschmidt's face was red.

"I know you didn't, Bill. Now let's plan tactics, as best we can. Any weapons, anybody?"

"I've got a pocketknife," said Monghetti shamefacedly. "I know it's against the rules to carry one, but when the shock came I was sharpening a pencil, and I forgot to lay it down."

"Forgiven, Harry," the warden smiled. "I've got a cool-gun—and a license for it. But I have only six cartridges. And I'm not the world's best shot. What's that you're holding, Smith?"

"Just a floor-hose nozzle, sir. I'm like Mr. Monghetti—I was just connecting the hose to wash down the floor of Ward E when the quake struck, and I carried it along without thinking."

"It will make a good blackjack."

"Not for me," said Smith complacently. "Here, Mr. Larson, you take it. I'd rather depend on judo."

The warden looked around him. The chairs, at least, were part metal, and heavy.

"The important thing is not to let them get into the office at all, if we can help it. There are 82 of them, and only six of us. At close quarters, enough of them crowding in here could simply overwhelm us. Here's the strategy. I doubt if they'll bother to break the door down, though of course they could, by sheer force of numbers; they'll get Farmer to open it for them. So it will be us in here, picking them off in the doorway, one by one."

"Like the pass at Thermopylae," said Salisbury. Nobody else but the warden recognized the allusion. He thought it an unfortunate one, considering that Leonidas and all his soldiers were slain.

He reached into a desk drawer, and drew out a little box.

"This is going to be the worst part, in a way," he said. "Waiting for things to start. Here, each of you take one of these."

"What are they?" Larson asked.

"Tranquipills. They won't affect you except to quiet jumpy

nerves. The doctor gave them to me when I—" He saw them exchange glances.

Larson and Groutschmidt shook their heads; everyone else took one. Morgan hesitated a moment, then closed the box and put it away. He felt perfectly steady.

"If we only had a paralymist outfit, or even old-fashioned tear-gas," Monghetti complained.

"Well, we haven't. That sort of thing went out with the old penal system. We're back to first principles now, man against man—six men against 82. I guess," he achieved a smile, "they forgot, when they passed the Bates-Watson Law, that California is an earthquake state. This is one contingency they didn't provide for."

He meditated for a moment. Which was better—to keep on talking, let off steam, or to let them use these last moments in silent strengthening of the spirit? Would that give them a chance to worry about their wives and children, make them jittery and shaky? He looked them over; they were a fine reliable lot.

"Let's not talk about it any more now," he said quietly. "Let's just get ourselves in position for the first assault. Groutschmidt, you and Salisbury are the strongest physically. What do you think about using these heavy chairs as battering-rams?"

"Could do," Salisbury said. Groutschmidt nodded.

"Then you two make up the first rank, right inside the doorway, with the chairs in front of you ready to grab. Smith, you stand right behind them, prepared to throw out anybody who gets past them. Harry and Ole Larson and I have the weapons, so we'll make up the backstop." He checked the gun and laid it on the edge of the desk, where he could reach it easily.

Then the wait began. Groutschmidt flexed his muscles. Salisbury, with a grin, sat down in his chair to rest, set to spring to his feet the instant there was a sound outside. Monghetti prayed. Smith took a picture from his wallet, looked at it a long time, and put it back. Larson turned and stared through the window, waiting stolidly for the first sign of life out in the yard.

And Miles Morgan had time to think.

He thought—when did he not? —about Laura, about their years together, about the anguish and shock of her death. He thought about his agreement four years ago to stay on in the work which had been all his life besides her. He thought about the understanding and sympathy of his staff here, all of whom knew all about his troubles. He thought about what must be happening right now in Ward H—unless they were already out of it. And he thought about that brilliant natural leader, that young, strong promising human being—that ineradicable, congenital, incurable criminal, whom a whole corps of psychiatrists had declared entirely sane, simply a throwback to the days of condottieri, corsairs, privateers—No. 30718.

He was 21 when he committed his final crime and when he began serving 50 years in San Quentin. In the ordinary way of things, the warden thought, he himself would have been long dead when 30718 came out, still apparently a young man, to a world of aged contemporaries—who would doubtless have to recommit him soon.

He never belonged to a gang or had any associate in his plunderings, though in his noncriminal life he was always foremost in every group. He simply took it for granted that everything he wanted belonged to him, and if anyone stood in his way he disposed of him. He had never had any conception of mine and thine—from childhood he stole as easily as he breathed. He would never have thought of being a pickpocket or a shoplifter or a sneak-thief—he simply took what he wanted when he wanted it, openly and directly. He burgled occupied houses and held up pedestrians and drove away in parked cars, and his speed and audacity and air of authority saved him from apprehension until the end. He was not greedy—embezzlement or forgery would have been distasteful to him, and he would not have known what to do with large sums of stolen money.

He would have made a wonderful Viking chieftain or leader of a Vandal horde or conquistador. Unfortunately he had been born into a world of peace, law, and order, all of which were completely alien to him. He was a pure atavistic mutation.

So natural was it to him to live and act as he did, that when by sheer accident his mother discovered, lying on his bureau where he had thrown it carelessly, a strangely set ring that she remembered described as part of the loot of a bold daytime burglary, and—a gentle but intrepid woman—accused him point blank, he calmly acknowledged his guilt.

"That's the way I am, mother," he said. "What are you going to do about it?"

He was then a senior in college, with an outstanding scholastic record. His home life could not have been better. He came of gentle, cultured people with high ideals, who loved him dearly.

His slight, shy mother faced him with agony in her eyes, but no fear.

"There is only one thing I can do, son," she said softly. "I shall have to tell your father, and he will have to turn you in to the police."

All this came out at his trial, on the testimony of a curious servant who was crouched at the keyhole, and who a minute later burst into the room, too late.

For the boy did not even become enraged. He smiled.

"Too bad, mother," he murmured. And sprang.

Before the screaming servant could reach them, his strong hands had twisted his mother's neck and broken it, as a butcher wrings the neck of a chicken. She had been a pretty woman. She was not pretty now.

The servant's screams brought immediate help, or she would have been next. A grocer's boy happened to be delivering an order at the back door, the next-door neighbor was gardening near the open window, a passing woman heard and used her wits, broke open the nearest police box, and summoned down a prowlcopter. Among them, the boy was seized before he could escape from the house.

Eight months later, after a long trial and many appeals, he became 30718.

And there was not the slightest doubt that, any minute now, he would lead the attack on the warden's office that had become a beleaguered fort.

Larson turned.

"Here they come," he announced.

"Watch till they get to the gate," the warden directed. "As soon as they find they can't get through and start back toward the building, take your positions and get ready. Is 30718 leading them?"

"It's hard to tell. Wait—oh, yes, I see him. He's standing over at the right; he's got them set up in regular military file. He's talking to one of them—it's Farmer, 29847. Farmer's supposed to get the gate open, I guess. He'd better not get too close—oops, he's found out. He's running back. Now they're talking again.

"Get set, warden. Conference over. They're wheeling, just like army drill. Here they come back. 30718 isn't at the head—oh, oh, he's marching in last. Real strategy there—shock troops first, I imagine."

"The guy ought to've been a general," Salisbury growled. He was the most recently employed of the staff members in the room, and knew least about the inmates.

"He ought indeed," murmured Morgan. "Well, here it comes. Watch for the instant the door begins to open, everybody."

But 30718 still had a surprise for them. They heard the tramp of feet in the hall outside. But there was no sound of tampering with the lock. Instead, a voice called through the door. Miles Morgan knew that voice; he had heard it last at the trial. Harry Monghetti knew it too; he had heard it when he stood by, waiting to turn on the freezer when the surgeon had deactivated the selected neurons in 30718's brain.

"We're coming in," said the voice, "and whoever's in there will be killed. We're giving you one chance. Turn the juice off the walls and gates so we can get away, and we'll go."

"You're not leaving here," Miles Morgan called back firmly. He felt an absurd impulse to add, "That's one more chance than you gave your own mother."

"O.K., if that's the way you want it. Do your work, Farmer."

It took Farmer eleven seconds by the warden's watch. The doorway at least was too narrow to be rushed by more than two men at a time.

They stood four abreast at first. There was no time for the defenders to notice who was who, but the big bruisers were in the van, the strongarm men, the muggers, the dangerous young who had murdered for thrills.

Obviously they had not expected any resistance. This will be a walk-over, 30718 must have told them; these guys won't fight. Perhaps he had expected the warden to be alone in his office to meet them all.

Salisbury and Groutschmidt swung the heavy chairs methodically, and for every swing a man went down. The defenders had one advantage—they were not freshly out of years of coma. The attackers' tactics changed. At a word from their commander they broke ranks and charged as a mob. Another after-shock made the walls tremble, but in the excitement of the melee it went unnoticed by either side.

Salisbury went down suddenly under a burly giant, who seized the chair and threw it straight at Larson. The heavy metal frame caught the chief orderly square on the forehead. Larson fell flat on his face and did not move again. Smith, crouching, seized the first comer by his ankles and threw him back at his companions. He got two more the same way, and then, before he could tackle the next, a fist caught him in the mouth and a knee in the solar plexus. He collapsed, moaning. Groutschmidt continued to swing like an automaton. Monghetti retrieved the chair and darted to Salisbury's place, but he was no equal to Groutschmidt. At a word from the invisible leader, half a dozen hands reached out for him and dragged him bodily through the doorway. He was passed overhead to the attackers' rear, and then the men in the room could no longer see him. They heard him scream once above the yells and panting.

Morgan sighted his gun carefully, aiming it away from Groutschmidt, now the sole defender at the door. He had only six cartridges. Larson had never even had a chance to use the hose-nozzle. Monghetti's pocket-knife had gone with him. The warden tried to estimate how many of the prisoners were left, but he gave it up. If any had been killed it would be by a fluke, and the injured would be getting themselves together and coming back to the fray. He shot without picking a target.

It hit somebody. There was a gurgling shriek, followed by a moment of surprised silence. Then the voice in back said coolly: "That's the warden—he's the only one who could have a gun. Go in and take him."

Smith began to come to his senses, but he couldn't stand. Monghetti was gone. Salisbury might be dead; Larson certainly was.

Morgan fired again, twice. There was no response; he had missed, both times.

Groutschmidt was beginning to give out. He had broken the chair by this time, and was wielding the heavy frame like a club. He brought it down on a head in the doorway, and the head disappeared. But an arm snaked past, and something flashed. The ex-prizefighter gasped and choked; a spout of blood splashed from his neck. Somebody had found Monghetti's knife.

Smith, crawling painfully across the floor, found Larson's

hose-nozzle. Groutschmidt's body was blocking the doorway. Smith reared himself up on it and struck. A leg was broken somewhere, from the crack and the screech. With his last strength Smith threw the nozzle back where it could not be seized, and they trampled him under.

There were three bullets left.

Salisbury opened his eyes. "My back's broken, warden," he croaked. "I can't move. For God's sake, don't let them get me."

Morgan's eyes fell on the technician, lying grotesquely misshapen like an eviscerated rag-doll. He nodded. "God bless you," whispered Salisbury as he died.

Now there were two bullets.

He had thought they would pour in at once. But the strategist at the rear was wasting no more of his men than necessary. Morgan could hear his commands. "Clear ranks," he ordered. "Drag all the casualties out of the way. You in front there, pull out those two who are blocking the door. Right. Now go in and get him."

Miles Morgan stood very still in front of his desk. His voice rang out through the doorway.

"I shall shoot dead the first man in," he said. "Who wants to be first?"

There was a vague stir. Storming the office was one thing. Sure death was another.

"Don't let him bluff you," sneered the voice in back.

"They know I'm not bluffing," said the warden. "You—30718."

"Yes?"

"You've got brains; why don't you use them? You know I won't deactivate the walls for you. You've killed five of my men; I don't know how many of yours we've got. Any minute now, reinforcements will be coming from outside. You can kill me, but that won't tell you where the atomic cut-off is or how to use it. By the time anyone could get in here without me, your wounded will have died of their injuries."

He raised his voice so none of them could miss one word.

"Some of you long-term men are mighty near the end of your sentences. You've made yourselves liable to new sentences of 50 years more. In other words, you'll all stay frozen till you die of old age.

"Every one of you knows I keep my promises. I give you my word I'll see to it that any of you who go quietly back to Ward H now and stay there will not be punished for this break.

"I shall give you just two minutes to turn and leave. Then, as I said, I shall shoot dead the first man in."

Morgan could hear his own heart beating. For a second there was no other sound at all. Then there was a shuffle, followed by a blow. "Don't be such fools," snarled 30718. "He's only stalling for time."

Just one, Morgan prayed silently, just one to lead the stampede!

He never knew which one it was.

When it had been quiet for a long time, except for the groans of somebody dying in pain back there in the hall, he went to the door and looked out, his gun steady in his hand. He knew there would be one left who was not a casualty. There was.

"Come here," he said. "You never were a coward, were you?"

"No, I never was," said 30718. He walked forward and faced the gun.

"You know that I have to do this," said the warden. The prisoner smiled.

"Sure," he said. "Law and order. They'd have stayed where they were, scared to death, if I hadn't egged them on. Well, we got some of you, didn't we? We'd have got you too if they'd only had my guts.

"Come on, get it over with. I guess that prosecutor at my trial was right when he said I was born in the wrong place at the wrong time. I'm what I am, and this isn't a world a man like me could live in and be himself. Shoot."

"Is that your last word?" asked the warden. "Aren't you sorry for anything?"

"Sorry? No—why should I be? If anybody stands in my way, I get rid of him if I can. I'm not a sentimentalist, like the rest of you. If I could grab that gun, I would. I can't. So let's finish it up."

Miles Morgan looked into the eyes of his son, and shot.

NOT SNOW NOR RAIN

On his first day as a mail carrier, Sam Wilson noted that inscription, cribbed from Herodotus, on the General Post Office, and took it to heart: "Not snow, nor rain, nor heat, nor gloom of night stays these couriers from the swift completion of their appointed rounds."

It couldn't be literally true, of course. Given a real blizzard, it would be impossible to make his way through the pathless drifts; and if there had been a major flood, he could hardly have swum to deliver letters to the marooned. Moreover, if he couldn't find the addressee, there was nothing to do but mark the envelope "Not known at this address," and take it back to be returned to the addresser or consigned to the Dead Letter Office. But through the years, Sam Wilson had been as consciously faithful and efficient as any Persian messenger.

Now the long years had galloped by, and this was the very last time he would walk his route before his retirement.

It would be good to put his feet up somewhere and ease them back into comfort; they had been Sam's loyal servants and they were more worn out than he was. But the thought of retirement bothered him. Mollie was going to get sick of having him around the house all day, and he was damned if he was going to sit on a park bench like other discarded old men and suck a pipe and stare at nothing, waiting for the hours to pass in a vacuum. He had his big interest, of course—his status as a devoted science fiction fan; he would have time now to read and reread, to watch hopefully from the roof of his apartment house for signs of a flying saucer. But that wasn't enough; what he needed was a project to keep him alert and occupied.

On his last delivery he found it.

The Ochterlonie Building, way down on lower Second Avenue, was a rundown, shabby old firetrap, once as solid as the Scotsman who had built it and named it for himself, but now, with its single open-cage elevator and its sagging floors, attracting only quack doctors and dubious private eyes and similar fauna on the edge of free enterprise. Sam had been delivering to it now for 35 years, watching its slow deterioration.

This time there was a whole batch of self-addressed letters for a tenant whose name was new to him, but that was hardly surprising—nowadays, in the Ochterlonie Building, tenants came and went.

They were small envelopes, addressed in blue, in printing simulating handwriting, to Orville K. Hesterson, Sec.-Treas., Time-Between-Time, 746 Ochterlonie Building, New York, N.Y. 10003. Feeling them with experienced fingers, Sam Wilson judged they were orders for something, doubtless enclosing money.

In most of the buildings on his last route, Sam knew, at least by sight, the employees who took in the mail, and they knew him. A lot of them knew this was his last trip; there were farewells and good wishes, and even a few small donations (since he wouldn't be there next Christmas) which he gratefully tucked in an inside pocket of the uniform he would never wear again. There were also two or three invitations to a drink, which, being still on duty, he had regretfully to decline.

But in the Ochterlonie Building, with its fly-by-night clientele, he was just the postman, and nobody greeted him except Howie Mallory, the decrepit elevator operator. Sam considered him soberly. It was going to be pretty tough financially from now on; could he, perhaps, find a job like Howie's? No. Not unless things got a lot tougher; standing all day would be just as bad as walking.

He went from office to office, getting rid of his load—mostly bills, duns and complaints, he imagined, in this hole. There was nothing for the seventh floor except this bunch for Time-Between-Time.

The seventh floor? He must be nuts. The Ochterlonie Building was six floors high.

Puzzled, he rang for Howie.

"What'd they do, build a penthouse office on top of this old dump?" he inquired.

The elevator operator laughed as at a feeble jest. "Sure," he said airily. "General Motors is using it as a hideaway."

"No, Howie—no fooling. Look here."

Mallory stared and shook his head. "There ain't no 746. Somebody got the number wrong. Or they got the building wrong. There's nobody here by that name."

"They couldn't—printed envelopes like these."

"O.K., wise guy," said Howie. "Look for yourself."

He led the way to the short flight of iron stairs and the trap door. While Mallory stood jeering at him, Sam determinedly climbed through. There was nothing in sight but the plain flat roof. He climbed down again.

"Last letters on my last delivery and I can't deliver them," Sam Wilson said disgustedly.

"Somebody's playing a joke, maybe."

"Crazy joke. Well, so long, Howie. Some young squirt will be taking his life in his hands in this broken-down cage of yours tomorrow."

Sam Wilson, whom nothing could deter from the swift completion of his appointed rounds, had to trudge back to the post office with 22 undelivered letters.

Years ago the United States Post Office gave up searching directories and reference books, or deciphering illiterate or screwy addresses, so as to make every possible delivery. That went out with three daily and two Saturday deliveries, two-cent drop postage, and all the other amenities that a submissive public let itself lose without a protest. But there was still a city directory in the office. Sam Wilson searched it stubbornly. Time-Between-Time was not listed. Neither was Orville K. Hesterson.

There was nothing to do but consider the letters nixies and turn them over to the proper department. If there was another bunch of them tomorrow, he would never know.

Retirement, after the first carefree week, was just as bad as

Sam Wilson had suspected it was going to be. Not bad enough to think yet about elevator operating or night watching, but bad enough to make him restless and edgy, and to make him snap Mollie's head off until they had their first bad quarrel for years. He'd never had time enough before to keep up with all the science fiction magazines and books. Now, with nothing but time, there weren't enough of them to fill the long days. What he needed was something—something that didn't involve walking—to make those endless hours speed up. He began thinking again about those 22 nixies.

He sat gloomily on a bench in Tompkins Square in the spring sunshine: just what he had sworn not to do, but if he stayed home another hour, Mollie would heave the vacuum cleaner at him. In the Public Library he had searched directories and phone books, for all the boroughs and for suburban New Jersey, Connecticut and Pennsylvania; Orville K. Hesterson appeared in none of them.

He didn't know why it was any of his business, except that Time-Between-Time had put a blot on the very end of his 35-year record and he wanted revenge. Also, it was something to do and be interested in. In a way, science fiction and detection had a lot in common, and Sam Wilson prided himself on his ability to guess ahead what was going to happen in a story. So why couldn't he figure out this puzzle, right here in Manhattan, Terra? But he was stymied.

Or was he?

Sam took his gloomy thoughts to Mulligan's. Every large city is a collection of villages. The people who live long enough in a neighborhood acquire their own groceries, their own drugstores, their own bars. The Wilsons had lived six years in their flat, and Mulligan's, catercornered across the street, was Sam's personal bar.

He was cautious as to what he said there. He'd heard enough backtalk already when he had been indiscreet enough once, after four beers, to express his views on UFOs. He had no desire to gain a reputation as a crackpot. But it was safe enough to remark conversationally, "How do you find out where a guy is when he says he's someplace and you write him there and the letter comes back?"

"You ought to know, Sam," said Ed, the day barkeep. "You were a postman long enough."

"If I knew, I wouldn't ask."

"Ask Information on the phone."

"He hasn't got a phone." That was the weirdest part of it—a business office without a phone.

In every bar, at every moment, there is somebody who knows all the answers. This somebody, a nondescript fellow nursing a Collins down the bar, spoke up: "It could be unlisted."

Sam's acquaintance didn't include people with unlisted phones; he hadn't thought of that.

"Then how do you find out his number?"

"You don't, unless he tells you. That's why he has it unlisted."

The police could get it, Sam thought. But they wouldn't, without a reason.

"Hey, maybe this guy's office is in one of them flying saucers and he forgot to come down and get his mail," Ed suggested brightly.

Sam scowled and walked out.

Nevertheless . . .

Nothing to do with UFOs, of course. That was ridiculous.

But suppose there was a warp in the space-time continuum? Suppose there had once been another Ochterlonie Building, or some day in the future there was going to be another one, somewhere in New York? There wasn't another now, in any of the boroughs, or any other building with a name remotely like it; his research had already established that.

Sam went back to the Public Library. The building, he knew, had been erected in 1898. He consulted directories as far back as they went; there never had been one of the name before. Then a time-slip from the future?

That was hopeless, so far as he could do anything about it, so he cast about for another solution. How about a parallel world?

That could be, certainly: some accident by which mail for that other Ochterlonie Building, the seven-story one, had (maybe just once) arrived in the wrong dimension.

He couldn't do anything to prove or disprove that, either. What he needed was a break.

He got it.

One morning in early summer his own mailbox in the downstairs hallway disgorged a long envelope, addressed to Mr. Samuel Wilson. The upper left-hand corner bore a printed return address: Time-Between-Time, 746 Ochterlonie Building, New

York, N.Y. 10003. He raced upstairs, locked himself in the bathroom, the one place Mollie couldn't interrupt him, and tore the envelope open with trembling fingers.

It was a form letter, with the "Dear Mr. Wilson" not too accurately typed in. It enclosed one of those blue-printed envelopes in simulated handwriting. The letterhead carried the familiar impossible address, but no phone number.

Maybe it was chance, maybe it was ESP, but he himself had got onto Time-Between-Time's mailing list!

He had trouble focusing his eyes to read the letter.

Dear Mr. Wilson:

Would you invest $1 to get a chance at $1,000?

Of course you would, especially if, win or lose, you got your dollar back.

In this atomic age, yesterday's science fiction has become today's and tomorrow's science fact. Time-Between-Time, a new organization, is planning establishment of a publishing company to bring out the best in new books, both fact and fiction, in the field of science, appealing to people who have never been interested until now.

Before we start, we are conducting a poll to find out what the general public thinks and feels about our probabilities of success. We're asking for your cooperation.

Our statisticians have told us that from the answers to one question—which may look off the beam but isn't—we can make a pretty good estimate. Here it is:

If tomorrow morning a spaceship landed in front of your house, and from it issued a band of extraterrestrial beings, who might or might not be human in appearance, what, in your best judgment, would be your own immediate reaction? Check one, or if you agree with none of the choices, indicate in the blank space beneath what your personal reaction would probably be.

1. Phone for the police. 2. Attack the aliens physically. 3. Faint. 4. Run away. 5. Call for assistance to seize the visitors. 6. Greet them, attempt to communicate, and welcome them in the name of your fellow-terrestrials 7. Other (please specify).

Return this letter, properly marked, in the enclosed envelope. To defray promotion expenses, enclose a dollar bill (no checks or money orders).

At the conclusion of this poll, all answers will be evaluated. The writer of the one which comes nearest to the answer reached by our electronic computer, which will be fed the same question, will receive $1,000 in dollar bills. Ties will receive duplicate prizes.

In addition, all participants, when our publishing firm has been established, will receive for their $1 a credit form entitling them to $1 off any book we publish.

Don't delay. Send in your answer NOW. Only letters enclosing $1 will be entered.

Very truly yours,
Time-Between-Time,
Orville K. Hesterson,
Sec.-Treas.

Sam Wilson read the letter three times. "It's crazy," he muttered. "It's a gyp."

What he ought to do was take the letter to the post office—Mr. Gross would be the one to see—and let them decide whether this Hesterson was using the mails to defraud. Let Mr. Gross and his department try to find 746 in the six-story Ochterlonie Building. As a faithful employee for 35 years, it was Sam's plain duty.

But then it would be out of his hands forever; he'd never even find out what happened. And he'd be back in the dull morass that retirement was turning out to be.

"Sam!" Mollie yelled outside the locked door. "Aren't you ever coming out of there?"

"I'm coming, I'm coming!" He put the letter and its enclosure back in the envelope and placed them in a pocket.

Time enough to decide that afternoon what he was going to do.

He escaped after lunch to what was becoming his refuge on a park bench. There he read the letter for the fourth time. For a long while he sat ruminating. About three o'clock he walked to the General Post Office—walking had become a habit hard to break—and hunted up the man who now had his old route, a youngster not more than 30 named Flanagan.

From the letter Sam extracted the return envelope.

"You been delivering any like this?" he asked.

Flanagan peered at it.

"Yeah," he said. "Plenty." He looked worried. "Gee, Wilson, I'm glad you came in. There's something funny about those deliveries, and I don't want to get in Dutch."

"Funny how?"

"My very first day on the route, I started up to the seventh floor of that building to deliver them—and there wasn't any seventh floor. So I asked the old elevator man—"

"Howie Mallory. I know him. He's been there for years."

"I guess so. Anyway, he said it was O.K. just to give them to him. He showed me a paper, signed with the name of this outfit, by the secretary or something—"

"Orville K. Hesterson," Sam said.

"That was it—saying that all mail for them was to be delivered to the elevator operator until further notice. So I've been giving it to him ever since—there's a big bunch every day. Is something wrong, Sam? Have I pulled a boner? Am I going to be in trouble?"

"No trouble. I'm just checking—little job they asked me to do for them, seeing I'm retired." Sam was surprised at the glibness with which that fib came out.

Flanagan looked still more worried. "He said their office was being remodeled or something, so he was looking after their mail till they could move in."

"Sure. Don't give it another thought." Another idea occurred to him; he lowered his voice. "I oughtn't to tell you this, Flanagan, but every new man on a route, they kind of check up on him the first few weeks, see if he's handling everything O.K. I'll tell them you're doing fine."

"Hey, thanks. Thanks a lot."

"Don't say anything about this. It's supposed to be secret."

"Oh, I won't."

Sam Wilson waved and walked out. He sat on the steps a while to think.

Was old Howie Mallory pulling a fast one? Was *he* Orville K. Hesterson? Had he cooked up a scheme to make himself some crooked money?

Three things against that. First, those nixies the first dav: why wouldn't Mallory have told him the same thing he told Flanagan? Sam would have believed him, if he had said they were building an office on the roof and giving it a number.

Second, Howie just wasn't smart enough. Of course he could be fronting for the real crook. But Sam had known him for years, and old Howie had always seemed downright stupidly honest. A man doesn't suddenly turn into a criminal after a lifetime of probity.

Third, if this was some fraudulent scheme involving Mallory, nobody the old man knew—least of all the postman who used to deliver mail to that very building—would ever have been allowed to appear on the sucker list.

Sam Wilson thought some more. Then he hunted up the nearest pay phone and called Mollie.

"Mollie? Sam. Look, I just met an old friend of mine—" he picked a name from a billboard visible from the phone booth—"Bill Seagram, you remember him—oh, sure you do; you've just forgotten. Anyway, he's just here for the day and we're going to have dinner and see a show. Don't wait up for me. I might be pretty late . . . No, I'm *not* phoning from Mulligan's . . . Now you know me, Mollie; do I ever drink too much? . . . Yeah, sure, he ought to've asked you too, but he didn't. O.K., he's impolite. Aw, Mollie, don't be like that—"

She hung up on him.

Sam Wilson stood concealed in a doorway from which he could see the cramped lobby of the Ochterlonie Building. It was ten minutes before somebody entered it and rang for the elevator. The minute Howie Mallory started up with his passenger, Sam darted into the building and started climbing the stairs. He heard Mallory passing him, going down again, but the elevator wasn't visible from the stairway. On the sixth floor, after a quick survey to see that the hall was clear and the doors closed that he had to pass, he found the iron steps to the trapdoor.

The roof was just as empty as the other time he had visited it. No, it wasn't. In a corner by the parapet, weighted with a brick to keep it from blowing away, was a large paper bag. Sam picked up the brick and looked inside. It was stuffed with those blue-printed envelopes.

He looked carefully about him. There were buildings all around, towering over the little old Ochterlonie Building. There were plenty of windows from which a curious eye could discern anything happening on that roof. But at night anybody in those buildings would be either working late or cleaning offices, with no reason whatever to go to a window; and Sam was sure nothing was going to happen till after dark.

It was a warm day and he had been carrying his coat. He folded it and put it down near the paper bag and sat on it with his back against the parapet. He cursed himself for not having had more foresight; he should have brought something to eat and something to read. Well, he wasn't going to climb down all those stairs and up again. He lighted his pipe and began waiting.

He must have dozed off, for he came to himself with a start and found it was almost dark. The paper bag was still there. It was just as well he had slept; now he'd have no trouble staying awake and watching. He might very well be there all night—in fact, he'd have to be, whether anything happened or not. The front door would be locked by now. Mollie would have a fit, but he had his alibi ready.

There was only one explanation left. Not time travel. Not alternate universes. Not an ordinary confidence game. Not—decidedly not—a hoax.

If he was wrong, then tomorrow morning he'd take the whole business to Mr. Gross. But he had a hunch he wasn't going to be wrong.

It was 12:15 by his wristwatch when he saw it coming.

It had no lights; nobody could have spotted it as it appeared suddenly out of nowhere and climbed straight down. It landed lightly as a drop of dew. The port opened and a small, spare man, very neatly dressed, as Sam could see with eyes accustomed to the darkness, stepped out. Orville K. Hesterson in person.

He tiptoed quickly to the paper bag. Then he saw Sam and stopped short. Sam reached out and grabbed a wrist. It felt like flesh, but he couldn't be sure.

"Who are you? What are you doing here?" the newcomer said in a strained whisper, just like a scared character in a soap opera. So he spoke English. Good: Sam didn't speak anything else.

"I'm from the United States Post Office," Sam replied suavely. Well, he had been, long enough, hadn't he?

"Oh. Well, now look, my friend—"

"*You* look. Talk. How much are you paying the elevator operator to put your mail up here every day?"

"Five dollars a day, in dollar bills, six days a week, left in the empty bag," answered Hesterson—it must be Hesterson—sullenly. "That's no crime, is it? Call this my office, and call that my rent. All I need an office for is to have somewhere to get my letters."

"Letters with money in them."

"We have to have funds for postage, don't we?"

"What about the postage on the first mailing list, before you got any dollars to pay for stamps?"

If it had been a little lighter, Sam would have been surer of the alarm that crossed Hesterson's face.

"I—well, we had to fabricate some of your currency for that. We regretted it—we aim to obey all local rules and regulations. As soon as we have enough coming in, we intend to send the amount to the New York postmaster as anonymous conscience money."

"How about the $1,000 prize? And those dollar book credits?"

"Oh, that. Well, we say '*when* our publishing firm has been established,' don't we? That publishing thing is just a gimmick. As for the $1,000, we give no intimation of when the poll will end."

Sam tightened his grasp on the wrist, which was beginning to wriggle.

"I see. O.K., explain the whole setup. It sounds crazy to me."

"I couldn't agree with you more," said Mr. Hesterson, to Sam's surprise. "That's exactly what, in our own idiom, I told—" Sam couldn't get the name; it sounded like a grunt. "But he's the boss and I'm only a scout third class." His voice grew plaintive. "You can't imagine what an ordeal it is, almost every week, to have to land in a secluded place where I can hide the flyer, make my way to New York, and buy a bunch of stamps and mail a batch of letters in broad daylight. We can simulate your paper and printing and typing well enough, but"—that grunt again—"insists we use genuine stamps. I told you we try to follow all your laws, as far as we possibly can. It's very difficult for me to keep this absurd shape for long at a time; I'm exhausted after every trip. I can assure you, these little night excursions from the mother-ship to pick up the letters are the very least of my burdens!"

"What in time does your boss think he's going to gain by such a screwy come-on?"

" 'In time'? Oh, just an idiomatic phrase. Like our calling our organization Time-Between-Time, time of course being just a dimension of space. I learned your tongue mostly from the B.B.C. and I don't always understand your speech in New York. My dear sir, do you here on this planet ask your bosses why they concoct their plans? Mine has a very profound mind; that's why he is the boss. All I know is that he persuaded the Council to try it out. A softening-up process—isn't that what you people call it when you use it in your silly wars with one another?"

"Softening for what?" But Sam Wilson knew the answer already.

"Why, for the invasion, of course," said Orville K. Hesterson, whose own real name was probably a grunt. "Surely you must be aware that, with planetwide devastation likely and even imminent, every world whose inhabitants can live comfortably under extreme radiation is looking to yours—Earth, as you call it—as a possible area for colonization? So many planets are so terribly overcrowded—there's always a rush for a new frontier. We've missed out too often; this time we're determined to be first."

"I'll be darned," said Sam, "if I can see how that questionnaire would be any help to you."

"But it's elementary, as I believe one of your famous law-enforcers once declared. First of all, we're gaining a pretty good idea of what kind of reception we're likely to meet when we arrive, and therefore whether we're going to need weapons to destroy what will be left of the population, or can reasonably expect to take over without difficulty. We figure that a cross-section of one of your largest cities will be a pretty good indication, and we can extrapolate from that. In the second place, the question itself is deliberately worded to startle the recipients, who have never in their lives contemplated such a thing as an extraterrestrial visitor—"

"Not me. I'm a science fiction fan from way back. It's all old stuff to me."

Hesterson clicked his tongue—or at least the tongue he was wearing. "Oh, dear, that *was* an error. We tried particularly not to include on our lists subscribers to any of your speculative periodicals. That wasn't my mistake, thank goodness; it was another scout who had the horrible job of spending several days here and compiling the lists. Under your present low radioactivity it's real agony for us."

"I'll tell you one mistake you did make, though," said Sam angrily. "You ought to've arranged with the elevator man before your first lot of answers was due. If you want to know, that's how I got onto the whole thing. I'm a mail carrier—I'm retired now, but I was then—and I was the one supposed to deliver the first batch. Mallory—that's the elevator operator—laughed in my face and told me there wasn't any 746 in this building, and I had to take the letters back to the post office—on my *last* delivery!" Sam couldn't keep the bitterness out of his voice. "After 35 years—well, that's neither here nor there. But I didn't like that and I made up my mind to find out what was happening."

"So that's it. Oh, dear, dear. I'll have to compensate for that or I *will* be in trouble."

Sam had had enough. "You are in trouble right now," he growled, pushing the little alien back against the parapet. "We're staying right here till morning, and then I'm going to call for help and take you and your flying saucer or whatever it is straight to the F.B.I."

The counterfeit Mr. Hesterson laughed.

"Oh, no indeed you aren't," he said mildly. "I can slip right back into my own shape whenever I want to—the only reason I haven't done it yet is that then I wouldn't have the equipment to talk to you—and I assure you that you couldn't hold me then. On the contrary. As you just pointed out to me, I did make one bad error, and my boss doesn't like errors. I have no intention of making another one by leaving you here to spread the news."

"What do you mean?" Sam Wilson cried. For the first time, after the years of accustomedness to the idea of extraterrestrial beings, a thrill of pure terror shot through him.

"This," said the outsider softly.

Before Sam could take another breath, the wrist he was holding slid from his grasp, all of Mr. Hesterson slithered into something utterly beyond imagining, and Sam found himself enveloped in invisible chains against which he was unable to make the slightest struggle. He felt himself being lifted and thrown into the cockpit. Something landed on top of him—undoubtedly the package of prize entries and dollar bills. His last conscious thought was a despairing one of Mollie.

Sam Wilson, devoted mail carrier, was making a longer trip than any Persian courier ever dreamed of, and not snow, nor rain, nor heat, nor gloom of night could stay him from his appointed round.

But he may not be gone forever. If he can be kept alive on that planet in some other solar system, they plan to bring him back as Exhibit One whenever World War III has made Earth sufficiently radioactive for Orville K. Hesterson's co-planetarians to live here comfortably.

THE MONSTER

They finally got Bobbie to bed, still sobbing, and they sat with him, talking to him softly until he fell into an exhausted slumber. They tiptoed out, leaving the bed-lamp burning, and practically fell into chairs.

Dick wiped his forehead. "We need a drink," he said.

Mary nodded, her eyes closed, but both of them were too tired to make the effort.

"Damned comics," Dick growled.

"Do you think that's it?"

"What else could it be? That or those horror movies and TV shows you let him see."

"Let him? All the kids watch them, and if you try to put your foot down, you're a cruel tyrant."

"I know, I know. And he's got to be popular, and adjust to his age-group, or we'll be raising a little neurotic. So now this!"

Mary shivered.

"It's like an epidemic," she said. "If it were just Bobbie, we could cope. But when every kid he knows—and when we can't even get the doctor, he's so busy with the ones whose parents got him first—"

Dick roused himself enough to get to the kitchen. He came back holding two bedewed glasses.

"Well, cheers!" he muttered. "Here's hoping it will be over as quickly as it began."

Mary looked at him over her raised glass, her eyes widened.

"Dick, I just had a horrid thought. Suppose it's really true?"

"Don't be a fool, darling. Anybody know that little girl's name? Any little girl reported missing?"

"No, but—"

"We've had the families of every kid Bobbie knows on the phone tonight, either them calling us or us calling them. Not a single one of them could tell us more than we got out of Bobbie."

"Lucille Devon said she'd heard it was a little girl on the South Side—"

"Sure; and when I called the police they switched me to somebody who's spent hours answering calls and saying automatically that no such report has been made. I'm sorry for them; they've had the devil's own time ever since school ended this afternoon, chasing the kids home from the cemetery."

It had started then. Mary wasn't taking Bobbie to and from school any more; at eight he was old enough to go the four blocks by himself. When he didn't come home by the usual time, she didn't worry—he'd probably gone home with one of his friends. Bobbie was a responsible child, and could be relied on to turn up by dinner-time, or else phone for permission to stay somewhere else.

Only he didn't; and when it was beginning to grow dark, Mary started calling the numbers of his special pals. After the fourth parent had reported no Bobbie—and no Martin or Kathy or Bill or Henry either—she began to worry in earnest.

Then Dick arrived, and even before he kissed her he asked, "Is Bobbie here?"

"No, he isn't, Dick, and I don't know where he can have got to. I've been phoning and—" An ice sliver stabbed her heart. "Dick, is something wrong? Do you know something?"

"Now, darling, calm down. It's just that crazy thing that was going on when I drove past the cemetery. I didn't think Bobbie could possibly be one of them, but—"

The old cemetery, which was due to be taken over and ploughed under for a new housing development as soon as the town could buy a suitable place on the outskirts to which to move the bodies, had once been on the outskirts itself, but now it was in the center of town; he passed it twice every week-day without even a glance or a thought. That was why he had given it a double-take when, this evening, he realized something peculiar was going on in it.

He slowed down and stopped at the curb to look. The cemetery, he could see through the main gate, was full of a running, screaming mob—and they were all children. As Dick stopped, the old watchman emerged from his little lodge, shaking his fist and yelling.

"What's the matter?" Dick called to him.

The old man shook his head.

"The kids!" he called back. "I don't know what's got into them! They came right over the wall. They've been pouring in here for two hours, and I can't get them out. I've phoned the cops—it's more than I can handle."

"Anything I can do to help?" Dick asked reluctantly; he was tired from the day's work and hardly felt up to dealing with a hundred or more screaming children. He scarcely waited for the watchman's gesture of negation before he started the car again and drove home fast to see if his own son was safely there.

Only he wasn't.

"Should we phone the police?" Mary asked dubiously when he had told her what he had seen.

"The watchman did that. I'm going to drive back there and see if I can find Bobbie. What in the name of heaven do you think has happened?"

But as he opened the door again, they could hear the crying. Down the street ran every child in the block, heading like homing pigeons for their own houses, every one of them, boys as well as girls, sobbing and howling. Mary ran down the steps and caught Bobbie in her arms as he hurled himself at her. They brought him in and she dropped with him into the nearest chair. Dick ran for a glass of water, the only thing he could think of.

It took a long time to get him quieted enough to say anything, and then it didn't make sense.

"The monster!" he kept crying. "It's in the cemetery! It strangled a little girl and ate her!"

"Shsh!" Mary soothed him. "That's just a story, Bobbie. There aren't any monsters. Somebody told a story and you thought it was true. Nobody's going to hurt you while daddy and mommie are here."

"It will, it will!" Bobbie sobbed. "The cops chased us away, and we were going to find it and kill it. It ate a little girl! They chased us away and now it will get out and come to people's houses!"

Dick tried another tack.

"All right, Bobbie. It's all over now. The policemen will find the monster and kill it for you. You don't have to be frightened any more."

Mary frowned up at him. "Better not," she mouthed silently. To the hysterical child she murmured, "Daddy means that *if* there had been a monster there the policemen would have found it and killed it. But we know there isn't any such thing as a monster that eats little girls, don't we?"

"There is!" Bobbie tried to leap out of her arms; she had to hold him tight. "Shut the windows! Please shut the windows, daddy! It'll come in and get us!"

"I don't like this, Mary," Dick said. "I'm going to phone Tallman."

But Dr. Tallman's nurse told them the doctor had been gone for half an hour. "I'll put your name on the list when he calls in, Mr. Frazier," she said. "But I don't know when he'll get around to you. He said to tell everybody who phoned to give the children a warm bath and some hot milk and put them to bed, and he'll check on them when he can."

"Could I get somebody else?"

"Not any child specialist, Mr. Frazier—they're all up to their ears in this crazy thing. Of course if your little boy isn't all right by tomorrow, Dr. Tallman can recommend a psychiatrist, if you wish."

"Certainly not," Dick snapped. "My child is perfectly normal mentally." He hung up.

There was nothing to do but follow instructions. At last they had been able to leave Bobbie worn out enough to sleep. The door to his room was open, and they could hear him if he stirred. Dinner was dried to leather on the stove.

He slept through to morning, though neither of his parents got much rest. At six, Mary slipped on her robe and slippers and made one of the periodic trips to his room. He opened his eyes and smiled at her. Then suddenly the eyes filled with terror and he clutched her hand.

"We've got to get the monster!" he whispered. He jumped out of bed.

"Dick!" Mary called. He came running, still half asleep, barefoot, his hair ruffled, and gathered Bobbie up in his arms.

"Steady, old man! Did you have a bad dream?"

"It wasn't a dream, daddy!" Dick could feel the child trembling. "We've got to get the monster!"

His parents stared at each other. Dick could feel anger welling up in him; he suppressed it with an effort. You couldn't be angry with a child obviously frightened out of his wits.

All over town, similar scenes were taking place. Something had spread like a plague to terrify every school-age child, and these children had infected their younger brothers and sisters, until babies barely able to talk were screaming in fear of a "mon'ter." The dividing-line seemed to be at 13 or 14; children of that age jeered at their juniors—but mildly. "Aw, you're nuts!" they scoffed—but their voices weren't steady.

The few children who went to school that morning were accompanied by parents, who promised solemnly to return for them at closing time. Teachers could do nothing with them: their minds were on nothing but the monster who had strangled and eaten a little girl whom nobody had ever heard of. Ridicule, scolding, persuasion had no effect. Principal after principal called the superintendent's office and asked what to do. They could not close the schools and send the children home; half of them would refuse to leave till their parents came for them, and the braver half would head straight back to the cemetery and another riot.

They would not get in again, however. The cemetery was guarded now, with embarrassed policemen every few feet around its walls. Among yesterday's frantic youngsters had been the mayor's son, and the two daughters of the chief of police. Shamefacedly the policemen had searched every inch of the cemetery, even entering vaults. There was nothing there but the peaceful dead. And still no one had reported a little girl missing.

The Fraziers kept Bobbie home. They kept their doors and windows locked, as he demanded, and gradually, after Dick had had to leave for work, he grew calm enough to unburden himself to his mother of what details he knew.

He wasn't sure which of the kids had known about it first in his class. But a note had been passed from hand to hand under Miss Schultz's unseeing eye, reading: "Look Out for the Monster!" Everybody had thought it was a joke. But then at recess all the kids began talking—he didn't know who was first, but soon everybody was telling everybody else.

The night before, everybody said to everybody, a huge monster, shaped like a man but with long iron hooks instead of hands and long iron teeth protruding from an enormous mouth, had risen up from the ground in the middle of the cemetery, vaulted the eight-foot wall, and escaped into the streets. It had slunk through alleys and behind buildings until it found a little girl who must have run away from home and was hiding in the back of an abandoned warehouse by the river.

When the monster saw her, it hurried toward her, swaying on its clumsy big feet, and gurgling horribly. As the girl caught sight of it, she screamed, but there was nobody to help her. She stood paralyzed by fear, unable to run, and the monster had grabbed her, strangled her with one iron hand, and squatted there on the empty sidewalk to satisfy its hunger. It had drunk her blood, then devoured her, skin and flesh and even bones, which it cracked to suck the marrow. All that was left was her hair and teeth and her clothes. Then, sated, it had lumbered back to the cemetery, and there it was hiding now, ready for another raid on the town as soon as darkness fell.

A lot of the kids laughed and made fun of the little ones who were scared. But as the story spread, with each narrator adding some detail to make it more circumstantial, even the skeptics began to get panicky. The trouble was, there was an answer ready for every question. How did anybody know about all this if nobody had been there but the little girl and the monster? Some boy had seen it, from a window of a building across the street, and had been too frightened to tell anyone till morning; then he had told other kids on the way to school. If he had done that, he must go to their school—so who was he? By this time nobody was sure who had told the story first. Why hadn't the cops found the little girl's hair and teeth and clothes, by this time? Maybe they had—or maybe the monster had hidden them or taken them away with him back to the cemetery. Well, then, how could the boy who was watching from the window know that the cemetery was where the monster had come from and gone back to? Because it came and went in that direction, and where else would a monster be able to conceal itself?

Then the bell rang and they had to go back to their rooms. In

Bobbie's class, Miss Schultz gave up in despair after a quarter hour of buzzing and inattention. "What on earth is the matter with all of you?" she cried; but nobody told her, because this was something that concerned kids, not grownups. Bobbie himself had thought perhaps she ought to be told—she could tell the cops and they would go to the cemetery and get the monster and kill it. He wrote that in a note to Jimmie Hayes, but Jimmie wrote back: "No, she'd laugh, she'd say we're making up stories. Let's *us* go. All of us, after school."

They were having a drawing lesson by then, and it was easy to pass notes. Jimmie handed his suggestion on, and everybody thought it was a swell idea. Other kids in other classes must have thought of it too; for the minute the closing bell had rung, there was a rush to get outside, where word passed from one to another, so that instead of heading for home the kids all dashed in a body toward the cemetery—all but a few sissies whose people came for them and who dared not ignore them.

The old watchman tried to bar the gate, but that didn't stop anybody. Some of the bigger kids swarmed up the wall, and helped the smaller ones over. They raced all over the place, trampling graves, knocking over bushes, finding not a trace of the intruder.

"But how did you think you could capture a—an ironclad monster, just you boys and girls, with nothing to attack it with?" his mother wanted to know.

"There was enough of us," Bobbie said curtly. "We could hold it, and send somebody to tell the watchman to get some cops. Anyway, pretty soon it wasn't just the kids from our school—the other schools found out and they came too, only it took them longer because they were farther away. One girl saw her cousin, from way over the other end of town."

"But you *didn't* find anything, did you?" She was going to add, didn't that show there was nothing there? when she saw Bobbie's lips quiver, and she bit the words back. Mass hysteria, mass panic—they weren't open to reason.

"It was hiding!" Bobbie's voice shook. "It knew we were there—it could hear us yelling and running. It hid.

"And then that old man called the cops anyway, when we hadn't told him to, and they came and they didn't even help us look—they just pushed us out of there, and left the monster scrounged down somewhere so he could come out again at night and get somebody else to eat! So I ran home as fast as I could, and—"

Then he started to cry, and Mary hastily took him into the kitchen and let him help her make lunch.

It was days before the town calmed down again. A psychiatrist from the city hospital and the head of the psychology department of the state university were called in for counsel. The two local radio stations and the nearest TV station donated time for them to broadcast analysis and advice. The daily paper made a big thing of it, with front page stories; then the wire services got it and it was a national sensation. A number of the more susceptible adults caught the fever from the children; there were commitments to mental hospitals, and there was even a woman who tried to gas her three children and herself, to escape the monster. A burglar too smart for his own good had the bright idea of disguising himself with false claws and fangs, was caught ransacking a house, and received a maximum sentence from an indignant judge. An unfortunate big man who had two artificial hands as the result of an accident was mobbed when he went downtown, and was only just rescued by the police.

The schools were shut down for the rest of the week. The police guard was withdrawn from the cemetery, only to be reinstated immediately when angry citizens jammed the switchboard with demands for protection for their children. The committee which was negotiating for removal of the cemetery held an emergency meeting and voted the funds to buy a site which the taxpayers had been complaining would cost too much, and to take steps for transfer of the remains.

Needless to say, even a second detailed search, inch by inch, had disclosed no sign whatever of anybody or anything in the cemetery which did not belong there.

The panic died as abruptly as it had been born. Two weeks later the children were "playing monster" and making a game of it, full of mock screams and giggles. They had a curiously self-satisfied air. Then the Christmas season neared, and they forgot even that.

Back in the small, squalid slum that strung its sordid shacks along the river, Tom Maginn lived on in his usual alcoholic haze. He snored on the filthy rags he called a bed, and roused himself only to stagger out and panhandle enough for another bottle. When he was hungry, which was seldom, he yelled for Tillie to cook something. When he realized after a long time that he never got an answer, he cursed and reeled over to the cupboard. He found some stale bread and a bit of cheese, mouldy but edible, gulped them down, and staggered back to bed. Damned obstinate kid, no better than her slut of a mother when she was alive, gallivanting around somewhere when her poor old father needed her. He'd beat her within an inch of her life when he got his hands on her. He fell asleep.

The cemetery was so old that nobody had been buried in it for 20 years or more. Before removal could begin, legal arrangements had to be made with representatives of the families who still had any representatives left. In the oldest part, against the back wall, most of the tombstones had long ago crumbled to ruin, or their inscriptions had worn away, and the yellowed records led to no survivors. It was the first part to be ploughed up; the bones that fell out of the rotted coffins were gathered together to be reburied in a mass grave in the new cemetery outside of town.

The old watchman, whose job would end with the removal, spent his days standing over the town workmen; he was a nuisance, but they were sorry for him and let him stay. His sight was still keen, and in the back of his mind was the thought that some of these people might have been buried wearing rings or other jewelry; it was his responsibility, and he had to make sure that if anything of the kind turned up it was put in his custody and not regarded as private treasure-trove until ownership had been established.

So it was he who spotted, in the shallow earth dug up from a long-neglected grave, a curious pile of oddments mixed with decayed coffin-wood and torn rags.

The watchman remembered the day two months before, when he had been overwhelmed by a mob of frightened children. But that affair had just been crazy, and was fortunately forgotten. He must be going crazy himself, to get such an idea. He pushed the stuff aside with his foot under a near-by bush.

Back in the shack beside the river, Tom Maginn was coming out of a long drunk. Soon he would start another; meanwhile he was getting his bearings and seeing things clearly again. What he saw was dirt and disorder and an empty cupboard.

"Tillie!" he shouted. There was no reply.

Maginn stumbled to the doorway. The sun was low, and the street was full of playing children; school had let out long ago. He tried to remember when he had seen his daughter last—hazily he recollected another time when he had roused himself and called for her in vain. He seized a passing urchin by the ear. The kid squealed and struggled.

"Shut up!" Maginn growled. "I ain't hurting you. Where's my Tillie at, do you know?"

"Leggo!" whined the boy. "How would I know?"

"You seen her today?"

"No. Leggo of me!"

Other children had trooped up, attracted by the fracas. The one he held wrenched his ear free and ran. Maginn turned to a little girl.

"You seen that damn kid of mine anywheres?"

The girl, poised for flight, shook her head.

"She ain't been to school, not for weeks and weeks."

"Old drunk Maginn!" yelled a boy from a safe distance. "Old drunk Maginn!" another echoed. "Betcha she run away from you!"

Then they were all shouting at him. He began to weep, tears of self-pity running down his grimy, unshaven cheeks.

"Damned disobedient slut's run away and left me! Left her poor old father all alone!" He sank down on the broken doorstep, sobbing. Delighted, the children whooped with glee. Soon they grew tired of watching the sodden man on the doorstep, and ran off to find other interests. After a while Maginn picked himself up and slammed the door behind him. If she was gone she was gone—her mother had gone before her, the same way—and that was that. He'd get along fine without her—sure he would.

It never even entered his head to report her missing.

At five o'clock the workmen in the cemetery called it a day. The old watchman prepared to lock the gates—the tools were put away already in his little lodge—and follow them. But first he took the heavy paper shopping-bag in which he had brought his lunch, and hobbled back to the grave by the wall. He fished up gingerly the heap of stuff he had hidden, and placed it carefully in the bag. Then he trudged back to the lodge.

Bobbie Frazier came home for lunch, and because it was Saturday found his father there too. Over hot dogs and coleslaw his parents discussed their week-end plans. Dick Frazier smiled down at his tousle-headed son.

"And what have *you* been doing all morning?" he inquired genially.

"Just playing with Jimmie." Bobbie swallowed half a glass of milk at a gulp and forgot to wipe his mouth. "You know something? That old man down at the cemetery, he's *mean!*"

"Old Tim Wallace? He's been around since I was a kid, and he always seemed good-natured to me. What did he do?"

"Jimmie and me wanted to slide on the big pile of dirt there by the gate, and he wouldn't let us."

"He was perfectly right. It might slip and hurt you."

"That wasn't what he said. He said, 'Scram, you two, or I'll sic the Monster on you!"

Dick and Mary exchanged glances. "Oh, Lord, not *again!*" she exclaimed.

But Bobbie just grinned. "Scuse me, please," he said, grabbing a handful of cookies. "I told Jimmie I'd come to his house after lunch."

"You be back by five, now," his mother warned him.

"Sure, mommie. 'Bye now!"

The front door shut behind him. Dick stood up.

"You know what I'm going to do?" he said. "I'm going down there and put the fear of God into old Tim Wallace. He ought to have better sense than to revive that old thing, just when it had got completely calmed down."

"I agree entirely. Wait a minute, Dick, I'm going with you."

Wallace was in the lodge when they parked the car at the cemetery. As they got out he came to the gate, shading his eyes against the sun.

"Mr. Wallace," Dick called, "may we talk to you for a minute?"

"Sure. Come on inside, it's hot out here. Take the good chair, lady. What's on your mind?"

"I'm Mrs. Frazier," Mary said, "and this is my husband."

"Pleased to meetcher."

"Our little boy was down here this morning, with one of his friends, and you ordered them away."

"No place for them," growled the old man. "Darned dangerous, climbing up that loose pile of dirt."

"You're quite right; I'm glad you shooed them off. But—"

"What we object to," Dick interrupted, "is talking to them about that Monster scare a few months ago. We want that forgotten for good, for the children's own sake."

Wallace looked at them craftily, a queer smile on his shrunken lips.

"You from the police or something?" he asked.

"Of course not—I'm an engineer. We just don't want the kids to get hysterical again."

"O.K., I won't say nothing about it any more," the watchman mumbled. He glanced at them again. "Want to see something funny?" he asked softly.

"What do you mean?"

"Something I found when they were digging up a grave in the old section." He reached into the corner and brought out a paper shopping-bag.

"Dick—I don't know—" Something about the man's manner made Mary feel a little queasy.

"It won't hurt you, lady. It ain't alive."

"If you've found anything the police ought to know about, I suggest you take it to them," Dick Frazier said firmly.

"And have them say I was crazy? Here, mister, you say you're an engineer—one of them scientists. Take a look at this."

Dick threw a reassuring glance at his wife. He's probably a little nuts, Mary thought compassionately, all those years here in the cemetery.

One by one the watchman drew from the bag and laid on the deal table indistinguishable objects crusted with mud. There were splinters of wood, from some old rotted coffin, probably. There were shredded rags that might once have been clothing. There were splintered pieces of fragile bone—a lot of them. There was a wad of matted brown hair with part of it still in a pigtail.

A humerus and a fibia were almost intact; so was a collar-bone.

A broken lower jaw was full of neglected little teeth.

"It's—it's—" Mary clutched the table for support, her head whirling. Dick put his arm around her and held her tight. His face was grey.

"That's what I thought," said Wallace grimly. "What's left of some little girl, ain't it? Wait—that's not all."

A sharp piece of corroded iron. Some more bones—big ones.

"There's a lot more still under the ground there," the watchman said. "I looked."

Dick Frazier pulled himself together.

"Oh, come now, Mr. Wallace," he said heartily. "I can understand that it annoyed you to have us come and complain, but you oughtn't to have frightened my wife like that. It's all right, Mary; these are just from one of the old graves they've dug up—people who died and were buried 50 years ago."

"Oh, yeah?" said Wallace. "That what you think? Suppose I told you these was right underneath the surface, on top of somebody's casket? The pieces of wood came from that, I grant you. But what's this iron thing, like a fang?"

"How should I know? Part of the coffin, I should think."

"Huh. And these here big bones—what are they from?"

Mary gave a little scream.

"Dick!" she gasped. "Look!"

Soberly, they both stared.

The bones were bigger than human. They were badly gnawed, pitted with hundreds of toothmarks.

The little toothmarks of furious children.

THE VOYAGE OF THE "DEBORAH PRATT"

This story may be partly myth; I don't know. But Jemmy Todd was my grandfather's grandfather. My grandfather remembered him as a child, and heard him tell the tale many times; and I as a child many times heard my grandfather repeat it. Certainly Quashee existed; I have a painting of him with Jemmy. Quashee was Jemmy's factotum until he died, very old, some time before the Civil War, but he was always free, and they were more like companions than master and servant. Of course by that time Quashee wore ordinary clothes and had learned to speak English.

Jemmy was youngest and newest of the crew of the brig "Deborah Pratt," out of the Gold Coast for New Orleans, though her home port was New Bedford. He would never have been on the ship had Captain Pratt not been his uncle, his mother's brother. The ship was named for Captain Pratt's mother, Jemmy's grandmother, who had reared him since he had been left a double orphan at two. When she died also, before Jemmy was quite 16, there was a family conference, and Captain Pratt, who was home between voyages and who was now the only man of the family, agreed to take him on.

He was reluctant, but not because of the "Deborah Pratt's" trade. The trade was illegal by then, and there was always a risk that the ship might be overtaken and impounded unless they could heave her cargo overboard in time, but it had been a family business for 50 years, and nobody in the Pratt and Todd clans felt any compunction about it. No, what worried the captain was the effect of the African climate on the boy, who, though strong for his years and wiry, was too lean and high-strung. He could make himself useful around the ship well enough, but they had to spend months on the Gold Coast during the dickering, and always left some of the crew in graves behind them.

Nobody, of course, asked Jemmy whether he wanted to go; it was taken for granted in New Bedford that every boy lived only for the day he could go to sea; and if he had any feelings of his own about the family trade, he would never have voiced them, or been listened to if he had.

He weathered the stay in Africa all right, being toughened up by the voyage out. While Captain Pratt bargained with the chiefs with whom he had long-established trade relations, the men were at loose ends. There was nothing much for them to do, in the sweltering heat, but keep the brig shipshape, guard the consignments in the barracoons on shore as they were brought in, and drink palm wine and, if they were hard up enough, go into the bushes with some likely native girl. Jemmy was safe from their carousing; he was the captain's nephew, and besides that they felt for him a half-paternal, half-contemptuous concern. He was an appealing lad, tall and thin, with big long-lashed blue eyes and a mop of curly dark hair.

So he spent his days about the barracoons, watching the cargo come in, and it was there that he struck up an acquaintance with one of the early arrivals, a boy of about his own age, slim and hard-muscled and very black, named Quashee—one of old Chief Matayo's catch. His uncle was too busy to notice, and the men laughed. One or two of them had a speculative gleam in their eyes as they watched the growing companionship, but there were plenty of willing girls and nobody, however drunk he got, was stupid enough to take a chance with the captain's kin.

Neither lad knew a word of the other's language, and Quashee, like all the rest, was fettered day and night in the barracoon; but somehow they managed to communicate. Jemmy would spend hours, surrounded by black men, women, and children of all ages, squatting beside Quashee. They would laugh together over nothing, draw pictures with sticks in the ground, talk to each other by signs and gestures. There was nobody else around of their own age or near it, so they gravitated together. Jemmy made all the advances in their queer friendship; Quashee at first was sullen, angry, and very frightened, and it was a long time before he differentiated Jemmy from the rest of his captors. When the last consignment came in, and preparations began for sailing, Jemmy grew disturbed and frightened too. But he said nothing, just watched and thought.

He came nearest to protesting when the branding began. He watched, shivering, as the hot iron stamped the thighs with the company's mark. "Why must you hurt them so?" he cried to the man in charge. The man guffawed. "We brand horses, don't we?" he countered. "Don't fret your head about them, boy; they don't mind. We're easy on 'em. We know the women's tenderer, and we never brand *them* hard. You worried about your friend? We'll take it easy with him, too."

But Quashee was branded like the others, and all Jemmy could do was stand aside and shudder. He thought Quashee would hate him after that, but the African boy had sense; he realized that Jemmy was as impotent as he. He stood quietly without a quiver while the hot iron marked him as property, holding himself motionless to show he was a man. He caught Jemmy's eye and pointed to the tribal scars on his face and chest, as if to say that that had hurt worse than this.

They were all stripped naked and chained together for the march on board. Some of the crew shook their heads when they saw how many of them there were this voyage. Jemmy heard two of them complaining together. "Where'll we put 'em? No use trying to keep the hold just for men, the way we did before, and leaving the wenches and young'uns on deck under tarpaulin; there won't be room." "Cap'n says, put the women in leg irons too. We figure about 15 to 20 will die out of every hundred, anyway, and when they're overboard we'll have more space." They were busy handing out bits of canvas for the blacks to wrap around their middles, for decency's sake.

It was Jemmy's task to go down in the hold twice daily and distribute the food. Once a day each of the cargo got half a pint of water. They lay on the bare planks on their right sides, spoon fashion, their heads in one another's laps, their leg irons closely meshed. There would have been no room for them otherwise. The sight and smell of them, the noise of their groans and lamentations, turned him sick. He mustered up courage to seek his uncle out.

"Don't worry, Jemmy," Captain Pratt smiled, patting his

nephew's shoulder. "They don't feel it the way we would. Anyway, when we're well out we'll bring them up on deck once in a while in bunches and have them jump up and down in the fresh air for exercise. It's to our interest to keep them in as good condition as we can—we want as many as possible alive, and all the live ones well, when we take them off in New Orleans."

"If they guess that, they might not be willing to help, mightn't they? Suppose they won't eat, or suppose they refuse to take exercise?"

"We set them just one example, and they get the idea," said the captain grimly. "Anybody that won't eat, and isn't sick, or anybody says he can't jump in his irons, we give him a taste of the cat. If he keeps it up after that, over the rail he goes; he wouldn't be worth the cost of delivering him to the traders. We don't usually have that kind of trouble more than once or twice a voyage.

"Now you go about your business, boy, and don't bother me any more. Time you grew up and got some sense. Where do you think the money came from that's supported you and your aunts and cousins all these years?"

Jemmy went away, deep in troubled thought.

His very first time in the hold, he had searched for Quashee and found him. There wasn't much he could do, but that little he did. He got his friend moved to a place against a bulkhead, where at least nobody crowded him from the front, and he risked giving Quashee a little more food and a little more water than anyone else got. The African boy realized very well what he was doing. When Jemmy came up to him, he smiled and pressed his hand. Jemmy was making a plan, and he wished he could tell Quashee about it. He didn't suppose he'd get any wages for his work, but he was a member of the family and so entitled to his share, in trust anyway, of the profits. When they reached New Orleans he determined to brave his uncle and ask that Quashee be bought for him in lieu of a cash return. Better keep on the good side of Uncle Pratt till then.

One morning, handing out the food ration, Jemmy noticed a man with his eyelids swollen and matted together as if with glue. He was rubbing at them and moaning with pain.

The next day there were half a dozen of them, and the day after that at least 30.

There was a ship's surgeon—when he was sober; but even drunk he felt affronted to be called upon to investigate the ailments of the animal cargo. Captain Pratt ordered him down all the same; how could he sell sore-eyed specimens like these? After a few days the doctor surlily obeyed.

He poked around in the hold and came up with his nose in a handkerchief.

"Epidemic muco-purulent ophthalmia," he said curtly. "They've all got it from each other or will soon, lying cheek to jowl like that."

"Can't you do something so they'll be cured by the time we land?"

"Do what? Smear ointment on them, if I had any, which I haven't? Most of them are ulcerated by now. No cure."

"You mean, they're going blind?"

"All of them, pretty soon, I'd say."

Only one was saved. Jemmy watched over Quashee, with his face to the bulkhead. Quashee's eyes remained clear.

Frantic, Captain Pratt ordered them all brought on deck, to see what fresh air might do for them.

The surgeon supervised the transfer. The first mate, with two husky sailors and Jemmy to help them, pulled the blacks to their feet and shoved and hustled them to the ladder. "Don't touch your hands to your eyes, men!" the surgeon kept warning them. "Wash your hands thoroughly before you touch your eyes!"

The Africans stumbled and moaned. Most of them by now seemed entirely blind. Those who could open their eyes at all showed blood-shot whites and sores running with thick, sticky, yellow mucus.

Still shackled by their leg irons, they were stood in rows on the upper deck. There was a stiff wind blowing, and the sea was restless.

The young ones, huddled on deck under the tarpaulin, made a concerted rush for their elders. Children dashed into their mothers' arms. The sailors, herding their charges like sheep dogs, were powerless to prevent them.

"Get them away!" yelled the captain. "They'll infect the whole lot!"

It was too late. Jemmy, bringing up the rear, lagging behind to shepherd Quashee, stood with his friend at the top of the ladder and saw it all. "The poor wretches must have agreed together as to what they should do," he used to tell my grandfather.

The minute they were in the open air and reunited with their children, they locked their arms together. And, irresistible by reason of numbers, holding the children to them, they moved as one to the rail and threw themselves into the ocean beneath them.

The helpless crew, panicky and getting in one another's way, could do nothing. One or two made to throw themselves after and pull the escapers back, but their comrades pushed them off the rail. Ominous sharp fins began to converge from all directions. One by one the black heads struggled and sank or were tugged under.

"Most horrible of all," Jemmy would say, "as they struck the sea they burst into song—a hymn, a chant to their heathen gods, I know not what—and the last one went down singing as we gazed."

Captain Pratt stood silent, watching the entire profit of his voyage disappear into the Atlantic Ocean. Only Quashee, standing with Jemmy at the open hatch, was left of the entire cargo.

"What did you think then?" my grandfather would ask.

"Only that now I should never be given a chance to bid for Quashee at any price I could raise. But it turned out otherwise."

The captain turned bitterly to the surgeon.

"Why?" he barked, as if the man who had herded the blacks on deck at his own order were responsible for what had become of them.

The surgeon smiled cruelly.

"They suffered from a disease," he said.

"I know. They were blind. But some of them could have been cured and sold without this utter loss."

"They suffered from still another disease," the surgeon retorted. "It is a disease called nostalgia, caused by their longing to return to their native land."

He turned toward the stricken sailors—poor devils, they too were victims. Most of them had had their choice between starvation and shipping on a slaver. Now what pay could they expect and what would be their future?

"Remember what I told you," said the surgeon. "Wash your hands well if you do not wish to bring the contagion to their own eyes."

He pivoted on his heel and strode into his cabin. He would be drunk and insensible now for days to come. The captain made no attempt to stop him; he was dazed with misery.

. . . Now, so far this is a fair and credible story, which I can well believe of those bad days. But the rest I cannot believe, yet Jemmy swore it to be truth.

Somehow some sort of order was restored, and since there was nothing else to do—they were past the halfway point of the voyage, and had he returned to the Gold Coast, Captain Pratt had no money now for further purchases—they set their course west-north-west as before. Somewhere in the confusion his uncle noticed Jemmy and Quashee—his sole salvage, a 16-year-old savage, but at least strong and well and with clear eyes. He did not ask why the black boy had not followed his compatriots; perhpas neither he nor Jemmy nor Quashee himself really knew.

"Leave him on deck," he commanded. "And you, boy, keep him in your charge. He is all I have left."

Then he too shut himself in his cabin, putting the first mate in charge.

So that night, a night of full moon and many stars, Jemmy and Quashee lay side by side on the open deck, and could see as well as by day.

According to the way my grandfather heard it and told it to me, two bells had just sounded, which would be one o'clock in the morning. Jemmy could not sleep, and had risen to pace the deck. The men of that watch were at their posts, and the rest asleep in their quarters.

Suddenly he saw in the moonlight two hands grasping the stern rail and a head following them. He raised a hail, and men came running and saw it as well. Two, three, four—ten of them in all, out of the hundreds who had gone overboard. It was impossible that they should have survived, still more impossible that they should have been able to clamber aboard again. Jemmy recognized one of them—a high chief's disobedient son, whom his father had sold in punsihment. Quashee had awakened and ran toward them. Jemmy pushed him back. He gasped a word in his native tongue, of which later Jemmy knew the meaning—the spirits of the dead.

They looked to be no spirits, but solid men, who threw themselves upon the gaping crewmen. The shackles were on their ankles still, and the irons knocked together as they ran. Yet afterward the sailors said they heard nothing and felt nothing, only saw. Whatever they were, they raised shadowy arms and tore with their fingers at the faces of the men they caught in that horrid embrace. Yet not one of them came near Jemmy, for Quashee stood before him and warded them off.

As quickly as they had appeared, they slithered to the rail again and one by one dropped off. In five minutes the deck was as empty as before. The men were panic-stricken. Some swore, some wept, some prayed, some grabbed at their eyes as if they pained them. The outcry they raised awoke all the officers and crew, and the captain came dashing out too. When he could get the rights of it, he cursed them all for a set of fools and cowards, and ordered them back to their posts. Gradually the fright subsided, but there were white faces and shaking hands to the end of the watch.

"Were you frightened also?" my grandfather used to ask.

"I was bewildered more than frightened. That night I promised myself that come what might, I should never go to sea again, and that somewhere, wherever I went and whatever I did, I should take Quashee with me, if I had to buy him with all of my inheritance, and set him free. For he had saved me from—something, I could not guess what, against his own people."

So Jemmy told it, and it was an unlikely enough tale. In his later days, when he was James Todd, Esq., a prosperous ship's chandler in New Bedford and a noted conductor on the Underground Railroad, he was reluctant to speak of it except to his young grandson who became my grandfather, lest his fellow-townsmen should think him mad. As for Quashee, though he was fluent enough in English by then, he answered not a word to all my grandfather's demands.

But this I can verify, for I have searched for it and found it in old news dispatches.

Three months after, a British barque, the "Wayfarer," found the "Deborah Pratt" wallowing in high seas in the South Atlantic, flying the flag of distress. Through glasses they saw the deck crowded with men. "They must be drunk or mad," said the captain of the "Wayfarer." "Hear how they shriek, and see how they stumble and throw up their arms."

Then a figure detached itself from the throng and staggered to the rail. It was, they discovered later, the surgeon of the

"Deborah Pratt."

"For God's sake," he cried, "do not board us. Make fast a line and tow us to the nearest port."

"What is it?" called back the "Wayfarer" 's captain. "What ails you? Have you some disease aboard?"

"We have indeed," the surgeon answered bitterly. "Except for two young lads, one white and one black, every man jack on our ship, from the captain to the lowest sailor—and including myself, God help me—suffers from purulent ophthalmia. It is one of the most contagious of diseases, and there is no remedy for it at the stage it has reached with us.

"We are all totally and incurably blind."

THE 1980 PRESIDENT

This is a glimpse into the hidden history behind history.

In August, 1980, Robert John Woodruff, Conservative candidate for President of the United States, did an utterly unprecedented thing. He consented to attend a top-secret, private meeting with his opponent, Senator Lynn Bartholomew, the Liberal candidate.

Both candidates, like the country at large, still felt a little self-conscious about the new names of their parties, arising from the Realignment Act of 1976, the Bicentennial Year. Both also felt self-conscious in themselves, for obvious reasons, being what they personally were. This departure from normal protocol, which ordains that rival candidates should never meet except for argument and controversy, was doubtless made possible for both of them by their own uniqueness.

That, and the fact that they were meeting at the behest, and in the seldom visited Washington home, of the Man in Brown.

The Man in Brown had a name, of course. He also had a very important and conspicuous governmental post, which he had held under changing administrations for twelve years. But he was known universally by his sobriquet—or sometimes as "the Brown Eminence" or "the Man of Mystery."

In a way he was mysterious, and in a way he was not. There was no mystery about his rapid rise in office. There was no mystery about his present post as head of the Federal agency dedicated, among other duties, to the protection of the president and vice-president. But his private life and his private past were completely unknown. He never alluded to them, and all he submitted to "Who's Who" were the date of his birth, a history of his official connections and his address in Washington. People said there must be something in his past of which he was ashamed. But it could be nothing shameful to himself, or he could never have been given his appointment. It was as if he had appeared, full-blown, about fifteen years earlier, and had never existed before then.

About his power there was no question. He did not issue any commands or give any orders. He was not authorized to do so. He merely assembled small groups of those who really ran things in each party. After he had talked to them they either followed his advice or were sorry they hadn't.

He was spare, not very tall, with thinning brown hair, mild hazel eyes and a quiet voice. His trademark and his only eccentricity was that he dressed always in brown, down to tan shirts and dark brown ties and shoes. Hence his nickname.

"My friends," he said on this August morning, with the air-conditioning screening off the oppressive heat, and with his guests settled in comfortable Figurmold chairs and supplied with glasses beaded with moisture and with the Inhalepruf Smokesafes that everybody had finally come to using, "no doubt you have been racking your brains on your way here—you, Mr. Woodruff, from your Foundation chairmanship in California, and you, Senator, from your constituency in Alaska—to to try to find some explanation for my asking you to this joint meeting. It was good of you both to make the trip without insisting first on knowing why."

Senator Bartholomew smiled and said: "We learned long ago in the Senate that if the Man in Brown wants to see us, he has a very good reason." Woodruff cleared his throat and added: "We've learned that outside of the Senate, too."

"That's far too kind," said their host suavely. "But this time it happens to be true.

"What I want to say to you both, in the presence of each other, can be put in very few words. Whichever of you wins in November will probably die soon."

"You mean, because I am—"

The two voices rose in unison and broke short in common embarrassment.

The Man in Brown looked at them quizzically.

"Because of your age?—no, not because of that," he said. "Though that was the real reason why both of you, though naturally you were both highly qualified otherwise, were nominated so easily on the first ballot—and also the reason that both your vice-presidential candidates are such outstanding figures.

"What I mean is—Let me say first that I attended both conventions."

"I didn't see you," said Woodruff bluntly.

"Nobody saw me. Except the few people I talked to there."

"The wheels behind the wheels?" inquired the Senator, with a touch of cynicism gained from years of public life.

"You might call them so. I told them what I am now going to tell you. In consequence, you two were nominated. But I also told them that I was not going to let either of you go blindfolded into danger."

"I'm used to danger," said Woodruff curtly.

"Not this sort. Be patient with me a little longer. I'll try to make things a bit clearer.

"I want to remind you of a strange phenomenon in American history. It is no secret—it has been published many times. It will be talked about throughout this campaign. I believe it is time to take it seriously.

"In 1840 William Henry Harrison was elected President. He died in office two months later. In 1860 Abraham Lincoln was elected; he was assassinated—not in his first term, but while in office. In 1880 James A. Garfield was elected; he was assassinated the following year. In 1900 the same sequence applied to William McKinley. In 1940 Franklin Delano Roosevelt was elected to this third term; he died in office during his fourth term. In 1960 John F. Kennedy was elected; he was assassinated before the end of his third year.

"Every twenty years, for 140 years now, the successful candidate for President of the United States either has been killed or has died of natural causes while in office.

"This is 1980."

There was a tense silence. Then Senator Bartholomew, very pale, murmured: "Other presidents have died in office."

"Only Zachary Taylor. And I'm not saying what has happened on other dates. I'm only remarking on what is associated with *these* dates."

Woodruff avoided his host's gaze. The Man in Brown smiled again.

"I know what you are thinking, Mr. Woodruff," he said calmly. "What both of you are thinking: coincidence, superstition. But have I a reputation for irrationality?

"I can't tell you *why* this has happened. Perhaps there is no reason, in any terms in which we can define reason. All I am pointing out is that it *has* happened every twenty years since 1840, and that it is now twenty years since 1960."

"They should have told us before the vote was taken," Woodruff muttered. "Your lot, too," he softly added to Senator Bartholomew.

"I know. I tried to get both conventions to agree to that," the Man in Brown said regretfully. "They refused. They were afraid nobody would be willing to run. It took all kinds of effort to get as much done as—"

"I see." Woodruff's tone was bitter. "I should have guessed. My campaign manager was the most surprised man at the convention—I was the darkest of dark horses, and I could scarcely believe my ears when I heard the votes on the first ballot. And when the man who had been the likeliest of all was nominated instead for the position of vice presidency—

"I'm a fool. My wife and my children will thank you for this!"

Senator Bartholomew, who was unmarried, nodded sympathetically.

The Man in Brown stood up and began to pace the floor of his austerely furnished living-room. He stopped abruptly and laid his hand on Woodruff's shaking shoulder.

"All this being so," he said, "are you still willing to serve?"

The Conservative candidate lifted his head. His dark eyes were somber.

"Of course," he answered. "My followers believe in me and the ideals I espouse."

"And I, for the same reason," said the Senator proudly.

The Man in Brown sighed in relief.

"That's what I've been waiting for you both to say. You're not just ambitious politicians, either of you; you're people with a cause—with two causes.

"All right. Now that's settled, let's see if there isn't some way by which we can manage to lift this curse."

EDITORIAL FROM THE WASHINGTON NEWS-POST-STAR, SEPTEMBER 4, 1980

This paper is not going to endorse either candidate for president this year. It is only 17 years since we Washingtonians had any vote at all, and we are not going to use it to condemn a fellow-being to death. Our advice to voters would be to stay home on the first Tuesday after the first Monday in November—or to vote only for other candidates than president.

Every citizen of the United States must know by now what is likely to happen to the candidate successful in 1980. We are not sure whether it was wise to give this matter such wide publicity, but that was the advice of high Federal officials. We, like every other communications medium, have obeyed.

There seems to be no way in which this crisis could have been averted. We couldn't change the presidential election year, or the length of the presidential term, because either would involve an amendment to the Constitution, which would require passage by two thirds of both Houses and ratification by two thirds of the States; and the 1980 election is now only two months away. The present incumbent couldn't be renominated and re-elected—even if he had been willing to take the risk—because the twenty-second amendment has not been repealed, and our president is now concluding his second term. We can't repeal that amendment in time, either.

So this paper has no endorsement to make for the presidency. We do have something to say about the vice-presidency. Both candidates are probably the most carefully selected and the most outstanding representatives of their party in American history. But in our opinion . . .

It was the strangest of all elections. Millions abstained from voting at all, and too many voted for a president they did not want, in the hope that their ballots might constitute a weapon of indirect murder. For the second time in our history neither candidate received a plurality. The election was thrown into the House of Representatives.

Then the Man in Brown appeared again. He consulted with a selected group of Congressmen, and suggested to them a brilliant maneuver. By means of every possible legislative stratagem, including the filibuster with no votes at all for cloture, the House delayed decision until 1980 was over. Their choice was announced the morning after the incumbent's term expired.

The new president (every American knows now which one it was, and how good a president the successful candidate became) had thus been elected in 1981.

Both Robert John Woodruff and Lynn Bartholomew, as we know, are alive and usefully active today.

But it had taken the Crisis of 1980 to induce the two major parties to nominate respectively a Negro foundation head and a Senator who happened to be a woman.

The weird fatality of the twenty-year periods will never menace a United States president again. In 1985, the twenty-eighth amendment to the Constitution was passed and ratified. All presidential elections are now held in years ending with an odd number, indivisible by 20. Of course a president may still die in office—but no longer by that inexplicable periodicity. Now, as we approach the end of the twentieth century, we look forward without trepidation to the election of 2001.

And some commentators have wondered if perhaps that repeated doom may not somehow have been *planned*—may not have had a meaning: the ending of deep-seated preconceptions, the final realization that human beings may be segregated by intellect or personality, but never by race or ancestry or sex.

In 1982, the Man in Brown (brown was a sacred color in his birthplace) reported to his superiors that the method had worked, the result was sure and his task was done. He urgently requested permission to retire at last and return home. His retirement took place after due notice, against all pleadings from the Administration to reconsider, and he promptly disappeared. No one on earth has seen or heard of him since.

The reason is simple. The superiors to whom he made his first, and activated, application were *not* on Earth. On a planet of another solar system he had been trained and prepared, and sent here to carry out the mission he had so ably performed.

With bigotry abolished in one great nation—and who knows what other missionaries are not at work in all civilized lands?—Earth is now one step nearer to eligibility for membership in the great Galactic Federation whose member-planets it will so soon be visiting.

THE PEAK LORDS

You may call this a confession if you wish. I prefer to call it a statement.

In the first place, I want it clearly understood that I am the legitimate son of a Peak Lord. I am neither a by-blow nor an impostor. This outrageous skepticism has to cease.

I acknowledge freely that I was vised Below on the date in question. But I was not there for any subversive reason whatever, nor was I there voluntarily. I deny emphatically that I have any compassion for the mutant dwellers Below, or that I was there in any endeavor to "help" or "incite" them.

Moreover, I was not there out of the morbid curiosity which impels students to don breathers and undertake anthropological or sociological research Below. I have no interest in the subhumans living there.

The actual fact is that I was kidnapped.

It was horrible, there Below. The darkness—the stinking soup that passes there for air—the throngs of mutant subhumans with their ground vehicles pouring yet more poison into the atmosphere that only they can breathe! And the streets full of crumbling, ruined buildings which they tear down periodically to make still more room for their vehicles! Some superstition must keep the mutants from taking over what were once the homes of real human beings like us, for they huddle in crowded tenements like so many nests of rattlesnakes.

I was so grateful when your people discovered me and took me out that I promised my rescuers rich rewards when I became Lord of our Peak. It was a dreadful shock to learn that they were not a salvage corps—my breather was almost exhausted and I had no recharges—but a police mission. I thought that all I should have to do would be to explain to you how and why I was there, and you would protect me, let me live in your Lord's court until I inherit. It is hard for me to believe that I am here as a prisoner, under judgment as a suspected criminal!

Do you perhaps imagine that I am one of those throwbacks—there have been some, I know, even in Peak Lord families—who condemn our glorious system, who have defected to the Below and set themselves up as champions of what they call "the oppressed"? Poor fools, how long could they last, unless they could find a quack doctor to give them the mutation operation (and often they have died from the doctor's lack of skill), or else smuggle in recharges for their breathers? I am no such idiot. All of them have died and been hailed by their subhuman "brothers" as martyrs to their "cause"—all of them, that is, who haven't been hauled back by their families in time and kept in close custody forever after.

I have no such death wish, I can assure you. I want to live.

Let me ask you another thing: how can you doubt, from the very mode of speech and manner which I cannot change or suppress even if I wanted to, that I am genuinely of a Peak Lord's family? You yourselves are all Peak dwellers. Can't you recognize my authority? I was born and reared in a royal household, just as your own Peak Lord and his family were. The vicious slanders I have seen and heard about myself in your communication media call me "arrogant." I say I keep the dignity taught me from infancy. Before whom should I be humble? There is no one on earth higher than the hundred or so Peak Lords and their families, dwelling as we do on the world's highest mountaintops, surrounded by retainers like yourselves who act as go-betweens to the mutants Below who serve the machines and produce the wealth, for the Peak Lords who own their territories and receive the wealth—and distribute a just portion of it to you. And I am a Peak Lord's closest kin.

My father's ancestors were among the first of the Peak Lords who staked out their claims when life gradually became unbearable in the poisoned cities, with their polluted air and water and their clouds of smog that shut out the sun. If you learned your history as children, you know that at first they were true pioneers, living the hard life of those who invade and transform a wilderness. They fought with others of their own breed to take and hold their Peaks, and they fought with the hordes from Below who tried to wrest the only unspoiled livable places on earth from those who had conquered them first.

By tradition the first Peak Lords were all experienced mountaineers; I know my own Founding Father was. Others were astronauts who could not endure grounding after it was finally learned that the other planets of our solar system were dead or unborn and uninhabitable by men. Gradually, as they and their followers won their wars and consolidated their holdings, each Peak Lord built up a civilized community and established control over the conquered Below in his own area. Then when the mutants appeared and spread—and don't think that was an accident; it was scientific research paid for by the Peak Lords themselves that brought about and evolved today's race of subhumans whose means of living depends on their productivity for our benefit—our present political and economic chain of command was established.

That is all elementary history, which you all learned in childhood.

You all know that those condemned to remain Below (and not only in the cities, as corruption spread to the countryside) died at first by the millions—and would all have died, had the Peak Lords not subsidized the intensive research projects—frankly, to protect their own sources of wealth. The dwellers Below had failed in all their own attempts to live underground or underseas, and they failed utterly in their feeble efforts to reconvert industrial plants or the nature of their vehicles to end the pollution. Only the Peak Lords by that time possessed the huge fortunes required.

Yes. Well, as I said, my father is descended from one of the very first Peak Lord families. Perhaps that is why, as so often happens in old families, he is an eccentric, strange, neurotic man. I should not dare say this if I were not out of his reach, for his anger is a terrible thing.

He is a lone wolf, who has never fraternized with any of his peers. That is why, when you took my case to your own Peak Lord, he said he had never seen or heard of me.

That is true. My father has never indulged in or allowed us—my mother and my younger brothers and sisters—any of the social visiting back and forth in royal air-processions which as you know are the custom of other Peak Lords.

He is a tyrant, and we have led miserable, lonely lives. He has never even tried to find us suitable wives and husbands as we reached marriageable age. We are all unmarried; when the last of us is dead the throne will go to a distant cousin. My father doesn't care, so long as he can keep himself alive and in power.

None of us has ever tried to escape—for where would we escape to? No other Lord would take us in (short of the secret refuge I ask for in my desperate situation), for fear of incurring my father's rage and perhaps precipitating violent action which would end the Planet-wide Peace Pact that has endured now for two centuries. Instead, they have quarantined us, and I imagine the young members of other Peak Lord families do not even know that we exist. Our Peak is far away, on the other side of the world.

Perhaps you think, when I say I was kidnapped, that I mean I really did try to escape?

No: in that case I should have chosen my destination, and it would not have been a Peak where nobody knows me and I am being treated as a common criminal.

I think now I had been given a counter-sedative to keep me from sleeping, while the servant who always sleeps at the foot of my bed had been given a draught to render him unconscious. I had never before had trouble in sleeping, but this night—is it only three nights ago?—I lay wide awake until I couldn't bear it any longer, so I got up.

But when I tried to arouse my servant to help me dress I could not shake him from his deep slumber, so I arranged my own clothing as best I could. It was the first time in my life that I had dressed without assistance—which may account for the accusation that I must be an impostor, because my clothing and ornaments are not arranged in regulation style.

I had a great desire—almost a thirst—to walk out in the open air. It was a bright moonlight night—so bright that I imagined I could even see the beacon of the abandoned atomic station on the moon.

Like all Peak castles, ours is a fortress too, still guarded regularly according to tradition although it is more than 100 years since any Peak Lord warred on another. I went quietly down the corridor leading from my rooms, to the first guarded door. Unusual as my action was, I knew that all I had to do was to explain to the guard that I wished to take a walk in the gardens, and to order him to provide an escort for me.

The guard was asleep.

It had never happened before, and I am sure now he too was drugged. He was liable to immediate execution, but I had no intention of reporting him. I stepped over his recumbent body and out into the tree-planted terrace. It was the first time I can remember that I have been completely alone.

I walked slowly under the trees, breathing the fresh cool air, my eyes on the stars that we had hoped some day to reach and now know we never can. I wondered if on some planet around one of them some other unhappy young man was walking and wondering as I was.

And then suddenly—I had heard no sound—I was caught from behind, and before I could open my mouth to cry out I was blindfolded, gagged and bound with rope. There were two of them at least; I am sure of that.

They dragged me over the garden to the outer gate. There too there should have been guards but no one stopped us. I was too busy trying to breathe to take much note, and when first I came back to my full senses I was lying, still bound, on a couch in a fast plane.

Through my blindfold I felt the rays of the sun and realized it was morning, but I had no idea of our direction or of the distance we had flown. I could hear men talking and they spoke the local dialect of our Peak. They said nothing that helped me; their conversation, such as it was, was only of the weather and of flying conditions.

Then I felt the plane swoop down for a landing. Hands unbound me, but left me gagged and blindfolded. I felt something clamped over my nose; I did not recognize it, but I found later it was a breather. The plane taxied to a stop, I was pulled to my feet, the gag and blindfold were torn from me, and I was given a rough push that sent me to my knees. By the time I recovered my balance the plane had taken off again.

I was Below.

It was some moments before my confusion enabled me to guess where I was. The sunshine of the upper air had vanished; I was in a sort of dingy twilight, and when I looked upward all I could see was an unbroken gray cloud. Through the breather I was able to inhale and exhale normally, but when experimentally I opened my mouth and breathed once through that, I was almost choked by the putrid miasma I took into my lungs.

Ahead of me from the landing field stretched a paved road, beyond which I could see dimly streets and houses. There was nowhere to go but forward, so I stumbled on and in half an hour or so the city had swallowed me up.

I need hardly tell you what it was like; you have visited it often, and you know.

It was horrible. I stumbled around those congested streets for most of the day, trying to avoid contact with the creatures that swarmed there. I ate nothing—how could I eat their food? I had no money in any case, and I couldn't understand or speak their dialect. They stared at me, but they're trained not to approach real humans, who are certain to be agents of their Peak Lord. The occasional scientist investigating, or the champions of the "oppressed," will approach *them*.

I grew panicky. With every minute my breather was running out, and when it failed I had no recharges or any means to get one. I would collapse and choke to death on one of those filthy streets.

And then I heard the copter, and I knew I had been vised and would be rescued. I was weak with relief and gratitude.

And your men told me I was under arrest.

Why won't you believe me? My father had me kidnapped and cast away Below to die. Why won't you take me to your Peak Lord or one of his trusted aides and let me prove my identity?

How do I know my father was to blame? Because I know my father. He hates us all—we are living reminders that some day he must give up his power and one of us will inherit it. But he has always hated me most. I am the eldest, and his first heir. And before he cowed me into terror of him, I was the only one who rebelled, who dared to answer him back, to try—vainly, I acknowledge—to sneak away sometimes for some sort of life of my own. You may say, what good would it do him to have me put out of the way? My oldest sister would come next, and there are five of us altogether. But that's just the point—I am the scapegoat, and because I am not the only child I am expendable.

Besides, he doesn't think the way sane people do.

So he decided to treat me as we treat our major criminals—I suppose you have the same system here—have me cast down Below to die.

I can't help it: the mere thought of him—I tell you, judges, my father was a wicked evil old man! I hated him. He deserved what—

Did I say "was"? I meant "is," of course—

I am too excited. I am weak still from my dreadful ordeal.

. . . No, I don't believe you. You are trying to trick me. My sister is too intimidated to have sent you any such message. Let me see it. I have a right to see it.

. . . I see. So all this time you have just been leading me on.

All right. There's no use keeping it up.

I was not kidnapped. It was I myself who drugged the servants and the guards. I fled in one of our swift flyers after I had surprised my father in his sleep. I felled him with his own heavy staff of office, with which he had so often beaten me.

I hid in your Below, as far away as I could travel, until you would vise me and bring me up, as any Peak Lord would do on vising a stranger without authorization in his Below. I threw away my recharges when I heard your copter start down for me. If I had dreamed what a Below was like I would never have had the courage to carry out my plan.

But I am *not* a criminal! It was not murder to destroy a tyrant! He deserved to die.

My sister is an ingrate. No, of course I never confided in her. But I relied on her; I was sure she would rejoice as I did when at last I mustered the courage to do what we all must have longed for—that she would gladly serve as Peak Lady until it was safe for me to declare myself and return. I would have named her as my successor.

Very well: let me go now. This is no concern of yours. I shall fly home again and take over from her.

No, you can't, you can't! There is no treaty between our Peaks. The most you have a right to do is to keep me as a guest of your Lord while he investigates! You will find out then that I am no murderer. I am a righteous executioner.

Take me before him and let me present my cause to my equal. What have I to do with your local laws?

. . . Sir! I did not realize! My father would never have sat in judgment in person at a criminal hearing—

No! No! I beg of you! I know your word is supreme in your jurisdiction, my Lord, and I know I entered it of my own volition. But—

Oh, dear God, no! Not without even a breather!

Kill me in any other way and I shall accept your judgment with the dignity worthy of my blood. But I implore you, my Lord, anything, anything—but not that dreadful city of mutants again!

Not—not— B
e
l
o
w
!

THE COLONY

They were not stranded. They were a deliverately planned colony of voluntary pioneers from an overcrowded planet which they—like the natives of every human-inhabited planet in every Galaxy—called Earth, or The World. They had selected this planet after scouts had investigated its terrain, its climate, its gravity, its atmosphere, the nature of its sun, and had ascertained the absence of any indications of an intelligent native race. They had been there 20 years. The first 250 had grown to more than a thousand, and children had been born who were now young men and women—and who thought of the planet, alien to their parents, as Earth, or The World.

It had been a hard life, but gradually they were taming the wilderness. They had cleared forest and jungle in the section in which they had landed because of its climatic likeness to their original home. At first purely agricultural, they were beginning to create a focus in a town that in time would be a city—in still more time the capital of a great nation, a city built then of stone and glass instead of wood. They had everything essential to most cultures except a cemetery—they cremated their dead and scattered the ashes. In another generation they would be able to declare the colony a success, and to send word (though it would take a long time for the message to reach its destination) that other colonies might settle elsewhere on the planet.

Their spaceship still stood on the charred ground where they had landed. Colonists whose only duty it was kept it in good repair. So fully stocked had it been with tools, seeds, all sorts of supplies to enable a civilized community to get started, that for a long time it had served as a warehouse or store-room; now most of its cargo was either used up or in use, but it was kept carefully ready to take off again if ever that became necessary. Rather soon the attendants began to take on the status almost of priests in a temple, and their maintenance job approached a ritual which the young people met increasingly with ridicule.

There had been many problems and difficulties, of course. There were the jungle and the forest, there were rivers (though, knowing that they would not at first be able to build boats, they had settled in the middle of a continent, far from any ocean). There were wild and dangerous animals. The one thing there was not—for otherwise they would, by their home-world Council's rules, have had to leave at once—was intelligent beings who could be considered the equals or potential equals of themselves. There were beasts that sometimes walked almost upright, and that communicated with one another by grunts and howls, but there was no question that these *were* beasts, not men.

It may have sounded like a strange and harsh ruling to compel them to evacuate the planet if they discovered any human or potentially human inhabitants. Couldn't they, one wonders, have come to terms with any such intelligent beings? Wasn't the planet big enough to be shared? But it was based on bitter experience. There had been other extraplanetary colonies planted by other overcrowded worlds with which their home, their Earth, was in communication. In every instance, any attempt at cohabitation by two completely alien races had resulted in catastrophe: either the colonists themselves had been wiped out, or they had been obliged to exterminate the original natives—and that necessity was overwhelmingly repugnant to a highly civilized people like theirs.

And then one day there came shambling into their little town from the far-off jungle a troop of some score of creatures of a kind the colonists had never seen before.

Like the beasts, these creatures were covered with thick hair. Occasionally they, especially the young ones, dropped on all fours and lurched ahead on their knuckles; but for the most part they walked upright, though round-shouldered and with their heads inclined to the ground. And they chattered. So did many of the animals, but this chatter sounded almost like speech. Aside from that, they had few characteristics of humans as the colonists understood humanity—they were quite naked, they performed the most intimate functions casually and openly, they grabbed food wherever they found it, and spat it out if it was not to their taste. But they threw stones and wielded sticks, and they made fires. They made them of the nearest fences.

The colonists' first reaction was spontaneous and inevitable. When the strangers moved into their fields and their streets, raided orchards and markets, met resistance with violence, there was only one thing to do, and that was to fight them off and drive them away. The colonists were a peaceable people, descendants of centuries of good, law-abiding citizens of a peaceful world, but they could not be expected to let themselves be looted, injured, even killed. At first, reluctant to treat these newcomers as they would have treated invading animals not on the borderline of humanity, they tried to drive them off with clubs, even to meet them with bare fists. But the strongest of them was no match for the immense strength of these creatues rather smaller than they; and after several young men had been left bleeding or with broken bones, and two of the older men had died of their injuries, they had no choice left.

They did not possess the most advanced weapons of their native planet, but they had been supplied with plenty of good serviceable firearms and ammunition. So far they had been able to deal with the wild beasts who threatened them, by means of snares and axes. But this was the emergency for which lethal weapons had been given them. Most of the guns were still stored in the ship; a party was organized immediately to get them and bring them back. Four hours after the nomads had wandered into the colony, the colonists gathered in a compact regiment and systematically started firing.

Three of the creatures fell dead, shot expertly through the head. The rest turned tail and dashed back whence they had come. There were mountains a few miles to the east of the valley which was now the colony, and the foothills were full of caves. Undoubtedly it was to these caves that the aggressors were fleeing. They had probably come from them, if they had not wandered from still farther away.

As they ran, one of them suddenly reached out a hairy arm, seized a frightened girl who was in their path, and ran on with his screaming captive held against him. Desperately the nearest men shot after him, willing to kill his victim too if necessary, rather than leave her to a worse horror. But the bullets missed him. The troop disappeared in the distance.

She was a beautiful girl, just 18 years old. Her name was Amritse; her father was a farmer on the outskirts of the town. He led the group that pursued the fleeing creatures, his face grey, his eyes staring, his gun triggered. But the colonists were soon outdistanced. They led her broken father back to his companions who were caring for their wounded.

Their own dead they cremated, as was their custom; but the three dead invaders they buried, as they did all inedible animals they killed. Only human beings were worthy of dissolution by pure fire.

When at last a shocked quiet had settled on the devastated colony, the Chief Justice, who was their highest official and by common consent their leader, called a general meeting in the largest building of the town—which for the present served them as auditorium, courtroom, school, and church. Even the nearest relatives of the two murdered men were there. Everyone came except the injured and Amritse's stricken parents.

And one other.

Where is Aghonizzen? the Chief Justice wondered, looking uneasily about him. Aghonizzen was his son, and his righthand aide. His wife was dead; Aghonizzen was his sole hold on a personal life. Now he was nowhere to be seen. The Chief Justice conquered his disquiet and turned to the assembled throng.

All over the hall people were clamoring to speak first. Firmly, and as soothingly as he could, the Chief Justice established order.

"You will all have a chance to give us your advice," he told them. "But first let us consider what questions we must answer in the face of this disaster."

"First, can we protect ourselves against a return of these invaders, or against another group of them? And how?"

"What about Amritse?" several voices yelled.

"I have not forgotten Amritse," the Chief Justice said sternly. "I hope and believe, poor girl, that she is dead. We have no idea how many of these—these beings there are; for us to leave our own territory, try to find them in the jungle or the caves, would be simple suicide, and have small chance of saving her. We must recognize her as lost, just as our two comrades whose ashes are still warm are lost to us."

Young people were jumping to their feet, shouting him down, waving their fists in the air. For a moment the Chief Justice was in danger of being mobbed and overwhelmed. Then the men and women of his own generation came to his rescue. Margotz, who had been pilot of the spaceship 20 years before; Envereddin, who had for a long time been the colony's only teacher; Lazzidir, its first doctor and now head of the small hospital, all bestirred themselves. Slowly they calmed the excited protesters, gained silence for the Chief Justice to go on. He felt drained and shaken, but he was not their leader for nothing.

"And the second thing we must consider," he said, facing them down, "is whether these are intelligent beings, however primitive. If they are, we should be violating Council law, to which all of us who founded this colony gave our unbreakable pledge, if we remained on this planet. We should be obligated to destroy all the evidences of our stay here, to activate our ship again, and under our instructions from home to set out again to search for a suitable world."

He shut his eyes and braced himself for the onslaught. He longed for Aghonizzen, who had the same charisma for the young as he had for their parents, who would have been able to control them and get them to think and talk logically about the problems before them. Where has he gone? he worried; and was afraid to let himself guess.

But this time there was no uproar. What he had said seemed to have struck his audience dumb. They sat and stared at him, young and old alike.

Twenty years of sacrifice and toil and struggle, their farms and their homes and their burgeoning town—all to be given up? The long, weary search to begin again? And what if at the end they never found a habitable planet without intelligent autochthons? Were they to return, old and worn out, to the over-populated Earth whose lack of opportunity had driven them out—where the vagaries of time would make that whole world a world of strangers, their relatives and friends long since dead?

It was the original colonists through whose minds darted that bleak prospect. To the young, natives of this planet, the whole idea was unbelievable.

"And I think," the Chief Justice went on, "that we shall have to decide the second matter before we can consider the first."

Under his calm speech anxiety gnawed. What had happened to the boy? Was he lying somewhere, hurt or dead? The last sight of him the Chief Justice had had, had been in the midst of the battle. But he continued speaking.

And little by little he persuaded them. Envereddin, Lazzidir, Margotz, others of the older men and women came to his aid.

"There is no need for immediate action," he said before he dismissed the meeting. "It is most unlikely that these invaders will return soon, after losing three of their number, or that another nomadic band will arrive suddenly. After all, in 20 years this is the first such disaster. Talk things over among yourselves, and in a week or so we shall meet again and come to some conclusion.

"One thing more I must say before we leave, and then I must go and see what I can do to comfort Amritse's poor parents. I know some of you hot-headed youngsters are eager to go in search of her. I implore you not to do so. It is most unlikely that she can still be alive, and you would almost certainly get yourselves killed. We have already lost enough, and we need you."

And as he watched the assembly breaking up, some of them still stunned into silence, others arguing and urging, he felt within him the frightened certainty that his own son had not waited for that warning.

It was six days later that he knew he was right. The Chief Justice's first act after the meeting had been to post sentries, day and night, both in the town and on the outskirts of the settlement—strong young men, fleet of foot to raise an alarm. It was a town sentry, late at night, who raised a cry. Exhausted, stumbling under his burden, dirty and ragged and with his hair matted with dried blood from a scalp wound, Aghonizzen staggered into the town. And in his arms he bore the unconscious girl.

At the hospital they sent for his father and for her parents. All he himself needed was first aid and rest and food. The girl was in much worse plight. Her right leg was broken, she had been savagely beaten and was a mass of bruises, and she remained completely unconscious. Aghonizzen, as he laid her down, gasped that until the day before she had been delirious, and she was in a high fever. He had had to gag her to keep her quiet, lest they be heard by her captors. The rest of the story, the doctor ordered, must wait. But after Amritse had been examined and cared for, Lazzidir was forced to acknowledge to her frantic father and mother that the girl had been repeatedly violated.

When the Chief Justice returned to the hospital the following morning, he found his son sufficiently recovered to be discharged. The boy still showed the effects of his terrible journey, but he was able to go home to his own bed and to tell his story, bit by bit, to his father. His first words startled the Chief Justice.

"I had to go," he said. "Amritse is my girl."

How little we know of what goes on in the minds and hearts of our children, thought the older man. He had been so close always to the boy, but he had never suspected. And under his surprise was a little glow; Aghonizzen had said "is," not "was." He would not have wanted a son whose love could be destroyed by the loved one's misfortune.

In short bursts—sometimes he even dozed off in between—Aghonizzen at last gave the whole account. He had started out only minutes after Amritse had been abducted, before any of the others, but even in his agony and despair he had kept his head. He knew there was no chance of rescuing her by force. The band was out of sight but their trail was clear, and at times he could even hear their blundering progress through the forest. Obviously they were heading for the foothills.

It was night before he caught up with them. In the moonlight they lay sprawled on the ground, sound asleep; even they worn out by the day's excitement. He approached cautiously, pretty sure they would have posted a sentry, and he had guessed correctly. Probably no alien could have the intimate mastery of this wild territory which the natives had, but Aghonizzen had lived always in a half-pioneer community, and he too knew how to walk noiselessly and stay unobserved. From a safe distance he watched, and as he expected saw one of the creatures standing by the embers of their fire. But search as he might, he could catch no glimpse of Amritse.

He watched all night, until they awoke and began to move on

again. Then he saw that some of them had slept, not on the ground, but in the lower branches of the trees. And he saw the heavy male who had seized the girl descend from a tree with her in his arms. She had been bound with tough vine-stems; he was not near enough to catch more than a bare sight, but he could hear her moaning. It was all he could do to hold himself back. But he knew any possibility of saving her would be gone forever if he showed himself now; he would have been torn to pieces instantly. In his haste he had not even armed himself; he had no weapon of any kind. As soon as they had picked up and started off again, he followed the trail.

In his night's vigil he had been able to get a better idea of the creatures. There were 14 of them, he knew now, counting three who had shared the trees with the abductor. Since three had been shot, there had been 17 who had invaded the colony. Eight of those left were children or young adolescents; five were adult females. The three the colonists had killed had been young males of about his own age. So the only full-grown male was the abductor himself, and he must be their leader, or perhaps the father of a polygamous family.

The implications of that sent a cold shudder through Aghonizzen's body, but there was still no way to rescue Amritse except by strategy. And now he realized another thing—the tying with vine-tendrils meant an ability beyond that of any lower animal: however unevolved or degraded, these were intelligent beings equivalent to man, and by Council law the colonists would have no choice but to abandon the planet.

But not without the girl, Aghonizzen vowed, unless he himself met death first.

It was on the third night that his opportunity came.

It seemed incredible, careful as he had been, that the sentries had not caught sight or sound of him. He slept by snatches, waking at the least noise. What food he ate was wild fruit or berries; he dared not light a fire, even if he had been able to snare some small animal. Thirst was beginning to tell on him when he came on them again that night, and found them camped on the banks of a river.

There were no trees bordering it large enough to bear the leader's weight. He lay snoring a little way from the rest of them. And Amritse, still bound and either asleep or unconscious, lay tied to a sturdy bush, by his side. The sentry this time was pacing the camp. Now, however, because of the river, he had only three sides to cover.

Aghonizzen watched him with straining eyes. Back and forth he paced, his head cocked for any sign of danger. The fire, which apparently they kept burning to ward off predatory beasts, was almost out.

He watched the sentry searching the ground for twigs to feed it. In this more open country, there were fewer of them than in the forest, and they had already used up what had been close at hand. The sentry turned his back and walked off a dozen steps. He began to gather wood, his head bent.

Risking everything, Aghonizzen took his once chance. Hardly breathing, he sped to the bush, swiftly untied the tendril that held the girl to it, lifted her slight body, and dashed away.

Fortunately she did not wake or cry; perhaps they had fed her soporific herbs to keep her quiet. So silent was he that the sentry was not alerted. Aghonizzen was almost out of hearing, and quite out of sight, before the sentry returned to his round and discovered the captive missing.

Then, as he had known would happen, there were outcries and hubbub, and the chase was on. Abruptly, stopping only for a deep drink of river water, Aghonizzen changed his course. Relatively intelligent these creatures might be, but they were no match for the tactics of a civilized human. They would expect him to return the way he had come. Instead, he went at right angles, making for the forest. As soon as he reached it he searched for a hiding-place. Light as the girl was, and now emaciated too, he also was near the end of his strength. It was in pulling her into the thick underbrush that the jagged end of a broken tree-branch slashed his scalp. There was nothing he could do about that but brush the blood out of his eyes until the bleeding stopped of its own accord. Holding tightly to Amritse, he fell into exhausted slumber.

When he awoke it was broad daylight. His first thought was of the girl. She was awake now, her eyes open, but there was no recognition in them. As he lifted her she whimpered in terror. His soothing words met no response. He must get help as soon as possible, or he feared she would die. He listened intently and heard nothing except bird-calls and the rustlings of small animals. He laid her gently on the ground and climbed the nearest tree as high as he could clamber. Between the forest and the invisible river there was no sign of his enemies. He climbed down again and, dread in his heart but urgency in his gait, hurried as best he could in the direction of the town.

"She will live," Lazzidir said. "Whether she will regain her reason I can't tell yet. But we can hope."

By the time the second meeting was called, Aghonizzen had recovered sufficiently to be able to address it. The Chief Justice's advisers had gathered in his house and heard the story first. A long discussion followed, and by the time the colonists had filled the auditorium the leaders' decisions had been made.

Every colonist able to travel was in the hall. They had spent a week of fear that the marauders would come again. By this time they were confident that there would be no expedition of vengeance. The memory-span of the aborigines was too short, the power of their chief too limited, for a renewed attack.

"There is no doubt that these are intelligent beings, sparse and nomadic as the population may be," Aghonizzen told them. "They are far too primitive and savage for us to negotiate with them; the only way we could maintain ourselves in safety on this planet would be by exterminating them. That, as we all know, and as my father has already said, would be a violation of the law by which we are bound. We made a mistake, however innocently, and we must pay for it."

A burly young man named Brogdin, bandaged still on both his shoulders, sprang to his feet. He was a troublemaker, and he had followers. But like any colonist he had a right to express his views.

"We are no longer bound by Council rules!" he shouted. "This is our world now; our fathers and we have worked for 20 years to build a home in it. I say, let's forget the old formalities and protect ourselves! These animals surprised us once and got away with it. It's not going to happen again, Council rules or no Council rules. Who'll join me in an armed campaign to hunt these creatures and wipe out all of them wherever we can find them?"

It was touch and go; there was imminent danger that Brogdin would stampede the meeting. It was Envereddin, who had taught them all, who saved the day. She raised her arms, and the tumult halted.

"We are civilized men and women," she said mildly. "We are not an invading army on this planet; we are peaceful colonists. The first-comers were all chosen by the Council and we are the representatives of an advanced society. We are not going to revert to the condition of the brutes we find now are the original inhabitants.

"Is that the kind of instruction I gave you young people when you were all my promising pupils?"

There was some shamefaced laughter, and the commotion died down.

To the Chief Justice's surprise, the next objection came from the oldest colonist—Megardis, whose husband had died in their first year, leaving her to work their farm alone.

"I am not satisfied, Chief Justice," she said, "that just because these creatures strike us with stones and clubs, or know how to tie vine-tendrils or kindle fires, this is proof they are fully human. On our own Earth we had apes who could do almost as much. But they were not classed as human beings, and we were free to kill them if they attacked us."

The Chief Justice glanced significantly at Lazzidir. Reluctantly, the doctor stood up.

"We had hoped," he said, "that I would not have to reveal this. Unhappily, we have absolute proof. So far, only the few most nearly concerned know about it. As many of you have had occasion to know from experience, one thing we brought from Earth, our home-planet, was the most advanced medical techniques and facilities. It is little more than two weeks since the attack on our colony. But the tests I have made are positive. Yes, these are human beings.

"Amritse is pregnant."

There were gasps and groans. Amritse's mother burst into sobs. And her father, his face ashen, said in a barely audible voice: "Our poor daughter has been driven mad by her terrible calamity. My wife and I would far rather see her dead than have this further horror inflicted on her. We are hoping to persuade Lazzidir to grant a peaceful death to her and—and the child."

The doctor shook his head firmly. But before he could speak, Aghonizzen jumped up.

"Listen, all of you," he cried, his voice breaking. "The child—yes. Lazzidir will know about that, and it is justified by our laws. But Amritse—I love Amritse, and when she was herself she loved me. Amritse is my chosen wife, whether she ever recovers or not. But she *will* recover—I shall cure her by my love and care, and she will be again what she was before, this dreadful thing forgotten.

"But not if we must stay on here, in constant danger of another raid by some band of these savages. My father and the wisest minds among us all say we must go, either back to the old home or on to find another. They have many reasons, and they are all good. But I, who was born here like so many of us, and have never known any other home, implore you to vote to go, for Amritse's sake if for no other reason!"

The vote was almost unanimous.

"Margotz," the Chief Justice said then, "you are in charge of our communication system. Exactly how long will it take to tell Earth what has happened and to receive their orders?"

The ex-pilot nerved himself.

"After our talk last night," he said, "I went to the ship. It is 20 years since our transplanetary radio was activated. I examined it with the chief attendant. It is no longer operative, and it is beyond repair with our facilities. We must make our own decision without instructions from home."

The Chief Justice gazed at him keenly. Margotz was the only one of them, except a young man he was training to be his successor, who had the necessary knowledge. It did not seem possible that the radio could deteriorate; but nobody could prove that Margotz was lying. Perhaps he was; perhaps he was among the many who were barricading themselves nightly in their houses and going armed about their work, in fear of a return of the savages, the many whose nerves could not endure the thought of months more of waiting until a message could be sent and returned. The Chief Justice was not sure he could keep his hold on the assembly if he accused so revered an elder of sabotage. His mind, conditioned to legality, was uneasy, but he decided upon the lesser evil.

"Then that's that," he said calmly. "We must make up our own minds. We shall proceed at once to pack our belongings and move into the ship. There were only 250 of us who came here in it, but it has a capacity of five times that number. Then we must systematically destroy every trace of our sojourn here. Some day thousands of years in the future these aborigines will become civilized, and they must never know that aliens from Earth, which to them is a far-off world under another sun, have ever come here.

"All we still have to determine is whether we are to seek another planet in another solar system where we can plant a new colony, or to return to Earth and either remain there or join another colonial quest later."

What he shrewdly guessed would happen came about. Most of the older men and women longed to die where they were born; the less adventurous among the young either were indifferent or were eager to exchange the hardships of pioneering for the amenities of civilization. A month later, their fields were bare, their buildings were leveled and the structural materials destroyed, their movable property was aboard the ship. The jungle would soon grow back in the clearings.

The first extraterrestrial colony on that planet had disappeared.

In 1979, by permission of one of the new African governments, a team of archaeologists from two European countries and the United States were undertaking a joint excavation under Professor Gundlichen, whose previous digs in the district had made it strongly probable that fossil remains of ancient man would be found there. In previous expeditions flint tools had been unearthed, and the remains of carbonized seeds and plants which, by the carbon-14 test, showed an age of approximately 30,000 years.

In the second month of the project, they made their first find. Gundlichen himself was in charge when a worker unearthed a fossilized human thigh bone. Slowly and with infinite care three human skeletons were uncovered, lying tangled together as if they had been thrown into a common grave. They were in a stratum still lower than the one in which Gundlichen had found tools and charcoal the year before.

They were all male, and young. They were of the Neanderthal type—the first of that race to have been discovered in Africa.

The skeletons were photographed *in situ* preparatory to their removal. Then the finicky operation began. Gundlichen bent down and inserted his fingers delicately under the nearest skull as soon as it had been freed. Nearly the whole staff was there watching.

Suddenly he turned ghastly white and dropped his find back into its resting-place. Pemberton, the British archaeologist, who happened to be beside him, caught him before he collapsed. The others hurried over.

"What is it? Is it his heart?" somebody asked. Gundlichen rallied and pulled himself upright.

"I'm all right," he said brusquely. "You!" he called to the native foreman. "Tell the men to stop work at once."

Phlegmatically the workers dropped their implements and stood aside.

"Go home," Gundlichen said. "Do not come back till tomorrow."

The puzzled professionals glanced at one another in perplexity. Gundlichen was their chief, but what was wrong? The old man achieved a smile.

"We'll go on tomorrow, ladies and gentlemen," he said suavely. "Something's come up that I want to study before we proceed further. Pemberton, and you, O'Brien"—he turned to his two colleagues—"will you wait here a minute? There's something I'd like to talk over with you.

When the three distinguished archaeologists were alone, Gundlichen seemed to have difficulty in speaking. He was still pale, and his eyes glittered.

"We shall of course apply the carbon-14 test to these bones," he said at last. "I have no doubt that we shall find these fossils even older than the material I dug up last year.

"So—what do you make of this?"

He stooped again and raised the closest skull. It rattled, and something fell out into his hand.

"O'Brien," he said, "look at the other two."

Completely at a loss for words, the three men stood staring at the incredible things.

Inside each of those Neanderthaloid skulls there had been a steel bullet.

THE CRIB CIRCUIT

She opened her eyes slowly; the lids seemed to be weighted down. All she could see was a white, diffused glare in which two human figures moved vaguely. She closed her eyes again.

A man's voice said, "Oak neow?" A woman's answered him, "Lil more."

Something hard and cold was pressed against her temples. She slept.

When she woke again it was day. Suddenly she remembered everything.

She was not in the container that with its maintenance had cost all she possessed. She was lying on some kind of bed, and perhaps this was a hospital room, though the crowded implements on the long table made it seem more like a laboratory. The two figures were there again, and this time she could see them plainly—a man and a woman, both naked except for white coats reaching to mid-thigh. They were both middle-aged; the man was clean-shaven, and he was completely bald; the woman's greying hair was sparse and cut short. The woman smiled reassuringly at her.

This time the woman was the one who said, "Oak neow?"

Alexandra tried to answer but no sound came out. A pang of fear shot through her; the cancer had been in her throat. The woman laid a hand on her arm.

"Doan be fraid, you can talk, juss weak."

With effort she summoned a whisper.

"Am I well?" she asked. 'Have you cured me?"

"Course. Not wake you till could."

She gave a long sigh. The terrible venture had paid off. In almost hysterical relief she burst into a long babble of explanation. The woman shook her head, still smiling.

"We know. Full file come with."

"What year is it? Can I get up and dress?" Suddenly she realized that she too, under a sheet of some shining fabric, was naked. "What comes next? Where is this? Are there—arrangements so I can find a place to live and get a job and—"

"Sh!"

"Sedtive?" the man asked.

"No need—juss react. Can you unnerstan her?"

"Hard."

"Call IBIS. They got someone."

He turned to the wall and dialed a small projection. In a few seconds the wall lighted up, and the face of a heavy-set elderly man appeared on it.

"IBIS," he said.

"Lo," the woman answered. "We got cryo case here. Time-speech trouble. You got"—she peered at the papers lying near her on the table—"twenny centry specialist?"

"Good," said the man on the screen. "Fine. Wait." He touched a button beside him—an intercom, Alexandra gathered. He spoke into it briefly, then turned back. "Send this affnoon—oak?"

"Oak."

"Thank for chance."

"*Our* thank."

The lighted wall switched off.

"Lil food neow—synthmilk. Tell them warm," the woman instructed the man. Apparently she was the doctor, he the nurse. She smiled at Alexandra again.

"Nice can swallow food?"

"Oh, yes!" A horrid memory of the last days swept over her—the agony, the drugs, the intravenous feeding until everything would be ready for her.

"Then you ress till affnoon, so strong nough to talk. Hard for you unnerstan our speech, hard for us too."

"If you'd rather use another language," Alexandra offered

timidly, "I speak two or three. Or is it just a different pronunciation because of the difference in time? You *are* speaking English, aren't you?"

"Mercan," said the doctor firmly. "*You* Ilan Inglis? We have Ilan Inglis nurse, you want?"

"Oh, no, I'm American too. I just thought—"

"Wait. Time-speech specialist come affnoon. Juss eat and ress."

The nurse reappeared with a tray on which stood a small jug of a silvery metal from whose spout a flexible tube extended. He touched a button and the pillow lifted. He tucked a plastic napkin around Alexandra's neck—was the scar still there? there was no pain—and held the jug while she took the tube into her mouth after a questioning glance at him and his nod.

"Suck," he said.

It was warm and strengthening, and she sipped it eagerly. The doctor turned to go. Alexandra took the tube from her mouth to call her back.

"Just one question," she said. "What is IBIS?"

"International Bureau Investigate Speech," said the doctor. "I be back." A door opened in the wall before her and she vanished. Alexandra finished the—what was it called?—synthmilk and the quiet young man took the jug away. He brought warm water, lifted the sheet and sponged her off. Alexandra felt herself blushing. He did not seem to notice. He touched a knob and curtains shut out the daylight. "Sleep neow," he said. He too went through the invisible door, bearing the washing equipment with him.

What was this, a sexless world? Or, on second thought, what was she—an old wasted skeleton that did not even suggest to the male nurse that she was a woman? She tried to view her body under the sheet. But there must have been a sedative in the drink; in half a minute she was asleep again.

The expert from IBIS was young—about her own age, 26, she guessed—and handsome, though he too was losing what had been a fine head of wavy fair hair. And he wore nothing but shoes of some plastic material and a small pouch slung over his shoulder. The doctor brought him in about half an hour after Alexandra had wakened. "Dr. Loren Watts," she introduced him, and departed.

"And you are Alexandra Burton," he said, smiling. He had a

nice baritone voice.

Alexandra looked surprised.

"I supposed by now you would all have numbers instead of names," she said.

He laughed. "We do all have numbers—one number we get at birth, which covers all our official connections—but we have names too, just like you. I might even be your remote descendant," he suggested.

"No, you couldn't; I've never had a child."

"Excuse me, I should have read your file first, but there was not time. Am I speaking correctly? Does it sound right to you?"

"Just a little stiff and formal."

"Ah, yes, it would be—I have learned your pronunciation only from early printed books of rhymed poetry. You must tell me when I am wrong. Of course, this is not my ordinary speech."

"Why is there such an enormous change?"

"My dear young lady, there is as much difference in the pronunciation of English—though we now call our dialect Mercan—between Eliot and Gardner (who is our contemporary poet of genius) as there was between Chaucer and Eliot."

"Chaucer died in 1400. Do you mean it is 500 years from—from my own time?"

"It is five-month 16—you would say about May tenth, I think—we have a 13-month calendar now—2498 today."

She felt dizzy. How was she ever going to fit into such a far-off age? But all she said was, "Has it taken them that long to find a cure for cancer?"

"Was that your trouble? It must have been bad, to kill you so young. We found cures for some kinds of cancer long ago, but apparently not for the kind from which you suffered."

"I see. Tell me, are there very many of us? I mean people who, from my own era on, were cryolized and now have been revived? Could I meet some of them and talk things over and find out just what things are like now and how I can adjust to my new life?"

Dr. Watts looked embarrassed.

"Nonposs," he said, suddenly reverting to his usual speech. "With mos of them, didn out-work."

"You mean, they couldn't be revivified?"

He nodded, his gaze evading hers. She noticed now that he wore contact lenses, and realized that so had all the others she had seen so far, either face-to-face or on the wall-screen.

"Then—oh, aren't there *any* others?"

"Some," he mumbled.

"Can I—"

"Burton, I am here to teach you our way of talking, and incidentally to advance my own knowledge of the pronunciation of your time. I am not competent for discussing other matters."

" 'Not competent to discuss'," she murmured.

"What? Oh. Thank you."

All at once she felt very weary.

"I'm afraid I must rest some more," she said. "You'll come again, won't you?"

"Every day, until we have learned everything we can from each other. I shall be here tomorrow morning. Shall I call your doctor now?"

"If you will. What is her name, by the way?"

"I do not know her, but she will tell you." He stood up to leave.

"Oh, just one more question—no, I'll ask her when she comes. I'll be seeing you."

"You will be—is that a colloquial phrase?"

"It only means 'till we meet again'."

"I see. Thank you. Farewell."

"Just 'goodbye' will do." But the invisible door had already closed behind him.

The doctor's name, she said, was Harris. She did a good many unidentifiable medical things to Alexandra, and discouraged general conversation; apart from the difficulty of their understanding each other, she had become curt, and Alexandra guessed she had been talking to Dr. Watts. So she refrained from asking the question she had almost asked Watts—why people in the 25th century all seemed to be nudists. Anyway, she had more or less reasoned it out for herself: it was May, warm weather, and undoubtedly even in winter the houses were kept warm. This obviously pragmatic society must wear covering outdoors against the cold when needed, but otherwise only such useful garments as shoes to walk on, hats against sunshine, and sanitary jackets or tunics for such occupations as surgery or chemistry. She would have to get used to it. They must have sex under pretty strict control.

It wasn't important. The important things were, how soon

would she be up and about again, and then how was she to live and make her living? The theory was that cryolosis subjects left money safely invested, which (even if a small sum) by the time they revived would have accumulated interest enough to provide a comfortable income. But Alexandra Burton, in despair at the thought of dying at 26, had put her very last cent into the freezing procedure and preservation of her remains; she was a pauper. And she doubted very much whether there would be any opening in 2498 for a skilled computer operator. They had probably passed way beyond that.

Dr. Harris was too busy (and rather too short-tempered now) to be bothered, at least today. Dr. Watts was coming tomorrow, and perhaps she could glean some information from him.

But he was evasive again. "This is not my field," he said. "I am purely a philologist. We were fortunate to get first opportunity at you—there are a dozen subsidiaries of CRIB and we have to take our turn."

"CRIB?"

"That is where you are now—in CRIB's hospital annex. Cryolosis Revival Investigation Board."

"Oh." She felt uneasy. An "opportunity" at her by a dozen agencies? Then when and how would her new life begin?

She was rapidly growing stronger. She was beginning to eat full meals again, which though apparently synthetic and the vegetables probably hydroponically grown, were nourishing, if fairly tasteless. In two days Dr. Harris had her first sitting and then walking on a balcony outside her room—from which she could see nothing but windowless buildings. The daily lessons with Watts continued, but it was patent that he was getting a great deal more from her than he was imparting to her in the way of understanding and speaking "Mercan." In fact, when after a week Dr. Harris told her she had an appointment next morning with the Board, the doctor added that Watts would come along to interpret if necessary.

There were two women and three men on the Board. They placed her in an oddly shaped chair (but theirs were oddly shaped too), with Watts beside her, and sat in a circle around her. The chairman, bald like, evidently, most men now but whose thin body hair was white, opened the proceedings.

"First we explain," he said. "Then you ask, we answer."

She didn't get much of the "explanation," even with Watts's help. What she did comprehend sent a quiver of fear through her. As Watts had told her, she was to be passed around in rotation from one subsidiary of CRIB to another, each one studying and investigating her in relation to its own specialty. But it sounded more like "treatment" than employment; nobody mentioned wages or where she was to live. Was this still her own city? It looked very different, even the little she had seen from her balcony. Was she still a citizen? Had she any legal rights or protection? But she bided her time to ask questions and listened in silence.

"Each branch of CRIB," the chairman concluded, "take care your board and lodge and make transport your next assignment." He pronounced it "assigh-ment." At least, thanks to Dr. Watts, he was intelligible.

"Oak?" he inquired of the other members of the Board, and they all nodded.

"Neow you have maybe quiries?"

Alexandra braced herself.

"What I want to know first of all," she said slowly and clearly, "is about the others."

"Others?"

"The other cryolosis cases. There must be some, or you would never have this set-up. Where are they now, and can I meet them and talk to them?"

The chairman looked, puzzled, at Watts, and he translated.

"Not many," the chairman said carefully, "and you first from so far back. Their time not yours. Wat good you talk to them?"

"Whether our pasts are the same or not, our present is the same, and I want to find out from those who have already experienced it just what our new lives are like."

Once again Dr. Watts interpreted, and this time he stumbled over "present" until it occurred to him that Alexandra had not been talking about gifts.

The chairman avoided her eyes.

"CRIB not set up juss for this—no, no! Only ten so far cured and revived, before you, none Mercan or Inglis but you." He waved away Alexandra's interrupting gesture. "And," he added, "six of them incomplete revivals."

"Incomplete, how?"

"Bodies cured and restored, but freezing not soon nough. Brains too long deprived oxygen. Minds gone—idiots."

"Oh," Alexandra gasped. Better not ask what had become of them; in all likelihood they were dead. She struggled for self-possession.

"That leaves four," she said desperately. "Where are *they?* I speak several languages—"

"Three still in rotation CRIB branches their own countries. One—finished circuit."

"And—"

The chairman turned to Dr. Watts. "Tell her so she unnerstan," he ordered. "She muss unnerstan." He burst into a long explanation of which she caught only a few ominous words. One cryptic phrase, "op pop," kept recurring. Watts looked like someone who had been commanded to do the impossible.

"Chairman Venable means—Chairman Venable is a very distinguished scientist. All the Board are highly qualified. It distresses them to cause you—disappointment.

"I shall have to explain fully. You are educated and intelligent, I know that from our association. I am sure we can rely on you to be sensible—you will realize—

"Ours is a very complex, super-organized, but smoothly running society. I imagine our general level of intellect is far above that which obtained in your—your former lifetime. When we are faced with—with obstacles to our planned progress, we have to deal with them realistically.

"The only way we can handle the multitudinous—that is the word?—problems of our social system is by establishing and adhering strictly to a rule of optimum population."

So that was "op pop."

"We can allow for no unplanned additions. Births must, by various arrangements, equal deaths. You cryolosis cases came here uninvited. We have no provision for even a small influx of unexpected persons. You cannot go back, of course, but it is not fair to expect us to destroy one of our own, or to deny our own people the right to have offspring so as to accommodate strangers from a much less scientifically developed period."

"That's specious!" Alexandra cried. "We are human too—we have a right—"

"You have no rights, only privileges, which we cannot afford to grant. I do not wish to be brutal, but I must be truthful. I will acknowledge—and I am only quoting Chairman Venable—that a few generations ago our ancestors made a bad mistake. We have of course always known of the existence of the stored containers, with their full dossiers attached to each. Incidentally, the practice of cryolosis ceased some 200 years ago; every one of you, revived or unrevived, dates from your time to about 2300. By that date the people then living had come to realize what cryolosis would mean to their descendants, and it became illegal.

"What our ancestors should have done was to refuse to treat or revive any of you. But the physiologists and the geneticists protested vehemently, and their lobby in World Government, which had become effectual two or three generations after your era, succeeded in securing a compromise settlement. As cures for the various diseases (including senility) from which you died were discovered, they were allowed to revive selected specimens—excuse the word, but that is what we were obliged to call them—you—but on condition that they should be maintained solely as subjects of scientific research. CRIB with all its branches—biological, historical, social, and whatnot—was already in existence, and was renamed and put in charge.

"It is hard, hard for us as well as for you. Some of you may be our own direct ancestors. So far, as Dr. Venable has told you, out of all those we have attempted to revive only five in all, including you, were restored to mental as well as physical health. In each instance we have had to explain the situation in a session similar to this one. It has been a terrific shock to each of the 'cryols', as we have come to call you, but in the end they have understood and accepted the conditions under which alone we can allow them to remain alive at all. We hope now that you too will understand and accept.

"Otherwise, we have no recourse except to—to return you to the extinction which should have been yours when you entered into this arrangement, for which we are not responsible."

Alexandra dug her nails into her palms in a frantic effort to avoid fainting. A Board member, looking at her with concern, pushed a button and summoned a robot bearing a sort of glass pump that sent a pungent mist swirling around her. She coughed and blinked and sat up straight again, her faintness over.

"Tell me the exact truth, Dr. Watts," she said directly. "I

understand what you have said so far; I can hardly agree, but I see your viewpoint. But you have omitted something, haven't you?"

"What?"

"When we—laboratory animals have made the circuit, when every branch of CRIB has studied us in turn and recorded its findings, what happens to us then?"

There was a silence. Then Watts said reluctantly, "There is no place for you. You are—we call it euthanased."

Venable, echoing the word, murmured. "You will be asleep. No hurt."

"I hate this!" one of the women on the Board burst out suddenly. "It is cruel. We should have let them all stay dead."

Numbly Alexandra noted how under the stress of emotion the slack pronunciation became sharpened.

"It is the law. We did not make it, but we muss obey it."

"Then," the woman said, "we should lie to them—let them think when CRIB circuit over they have new life like ours."

There was an agitated murmur among the other Board members. "Immoral!" objected one of the men. The chairman raised his hand.

"Plizz! Order! We discuss nother time." He turned to Alexandra. "Session over. You go now. Watts take you back to room."

Lying awake that night in her hospital bed, Alexandra mulled over and rejected possible and impossible ways of escape.

Suicide? What was the point of that, even if she had had the means? Death was what she was trying to avoid. There was no possible way of going back, of being refrozen; cryolosis was no longer practiced in 2498 and if it had been, she would have been the last person to be considered for it. For a while she played with a fantasy—Loren Watts had fallen in love with her, he would rescue her and take her away and hide her. That was nonsense; common sense told her that he was interested in her merely for philological reasons, and even if that had not been true, he would have wrecked his career by any attempt to save her, or even any protest. Running away, getting out of the hospital somehow and trying to lose herself in the city? How, without money, without a chance of earning any, and unable even to speak comprehensibly?

Then just give up as the others had done, acquiesce, submit and go the rounds as a guinea pig, and then like any other experimental animal let herself be snuffed out when her usefulness was over? Every fiber of her being rebelled against that.

Out of pure despair the first faint glimmerings of a plan came to her.

If somehow she had something, anything, with which she could bargain—

What? The various branches of CRIB would milk her dry of information about her own time, and inspect her physically and mentally far beyond her own powers of revelation. Her experience of computer technique would be child's play in the 25th century. The rather feeble Psi faculty she had possessed did nothing for her now except to have warned her faintly of trouble coming here.

This Orwellian nightmare which was the world of 2498 was frightening. If only there were some way to warn people of the 20th century! There wasn't—apparently time-travel was still a dream. It would have been better in the long run, Alexandra thought bitterly, to have died of cancer in 1970—as indeed she had done—and make an end of it.

Would it have made any difference if, like other people, she had been rich enough to invest surplus funds that by some miracle of accruing interest would have prepared a fortune for her when she was unfrozen? Everybody had advised her against devoting her last penny to the freezing and its upkeep; even the Cryology Institute itself had yielded reluctantly to her insistence. No, she had told them, I shall be well again, I am young, I have no one to whom to leave my savings, I can make my way somehow. So here she was, in as strange a world as if she had come from another planet, although presumably she was still in her native city. And its ways were not her accustomed ways, and if they used money at all, no money of hers could have come down so many years—or made any difference if it had.

One thing she was determined on: if she could devise a means of bargaining, it would not be to assure her a new lifetime of going for all her remaining natural span of years from branch to branch of CRIB. Either she must give up and die, or she must find a way to live free, as one of the citizens of this new world.

But how?

And then an idea came to her. It was preposterous, she could never put it over. She could not have done so even in her own primitive time. But any factual ploy was completely hopeless. So it was this or nothing.

She began to plan.

However mechanical, inflexible and austere this 25th century society might be, its members were still human beings. Their emotions might be suppressed, but they existed. No superego exists without an id.

"How much longer do I have with IBIS?" she asked Watts at their next session.

"About a week more, I think. Then you go next to HIP—Historical Investigation Project."

"Does each of them take about the same time?"

"Oh, no. When it comes to the physical, psychological, and genetic branches, they might take weeks, even months. The intellectual research programs like IBIS and HIP cannot take so long—they depend on what the subject knows consciously that is of any value to us, and this is not likely, except for the language differences, to be very much."

"I see."

So now she knew that her escape effort must take place while she was under investigation by HIP. Only these so-called "intellectual" branches of CRIB would be likely to be manned by human researchers; the physical examinations would undoubtedly be by machines.

That meant she must be able, by the time of her transfer from IBIS, to speak and understand "Mercan." She applied herself intensively to her side of the dialogue with Watts, no matter how hard he tried to tip the balance in favor of himself. By the end of the week she could understand most of the conversation addressed to her, or overheard, by doctors, nurses, and speaking-robot orderlies in the hospital, and could make herself fairly well understood in turn by them.

Dr. Watts bade her farewell with reluctance, but obviously only because he was not sure there was nothing left he could learn from her. Any dream of his personal interest in her was just that—a dream. Since she had never seen any other member of the IBIS staff, she assumed that in all the other branches also just one investigator would be assigned to her.

She was transported to HIP, wherever its quarters were located, at night and by a bewildering series of shafts and escalators and ramps and elevators. She found one difference when she arrived; she was established in a room and bath in an unspecified building, and told that her meals would come to her whenever she ordered them by operating a rather elaborate menu dial. A slide in the wall came out with the food—strange-tasting and apparently synthetic, on a hot plate. The bed and the bathroom fixtures, too, had peculiar features with which she had to acquaint herself by experiment. She was left alone for the rest of the night, and finally managed to drop off to sleep until chimes awakened her and voice from a grille high in the wall announced that a member of the HIP staff would arrive in 15 minutes.

The HIP researcher, to Alexandra's relief, was a woman. Not only was it still hard to accustom herself to the universal nudity, but the plan she had in mind might be easier to achieve on a female-to-female basis.

"I am Dr. Ann Mayhew," the historian introduced herself. She was young, good-looking, and had the brisk immediacy of all the scientific workers—were they all doctors of one sort or another?—whom Alexandra had met. She carried a kind of portable computer whose workings Alexandra, for all her own cybernetic training, found inexplicable.

"You are, from dossier, very well educated for your era," Dr. Mayhew said. Alexandra bristled at the faintly patronizing tone, but this was no time to arouse antagonism. "I begin, therefore, by ask you about several dispute points twenny centry history."

"I'm not sure," Alexandra began carefully, pronouncing the words as Watts had taught her, "whether I shall be able to answer your questions in terms that will mean anything to you."

"Why not?"

"Because in my day so much depended on—well, extraneous issues—"

"Extraneous? That means?"

"Outside—you might say irrelevant. You see, we are—we were guided very largely, even if only subconsciously, by motivations that arose not from logic or reason but from pure feeling, often from irrational emotions which we ourselves knew to be so, but could not free ourselves from."

"Barbarous! You mean you allowed such to guide your national and or international action?"

"I'm afraid so."

Dr. Mayhew was silent. She looked bewildered, as if not knowing how to go on from a standpoint she found incomprehensible. Alexandra waited. Finally the historian said tentatively, "You are right, it will be hard. But we try. For examp—"

"Wait!" cried Alexandra suddenly. She felt a little light-headed; there was every possibility that in a few minutes she might be cut short and ordered liquidated as mentally unsound. But it was now or never.

She braced herself.

"Before you start," she said, "tell me one thing: do you want the official history, or the real history?"

"You mean not the same?"

"Of course not. I told you we were guided largely by feeling rather than by reason. There was a thing we used to call the credibility gap. In other words, those in power often lied to the public, because they feared that if they told the truth, the result might be panic, perhaps total chaos if it couldn't be stopped in time."

Dr. Mayhew frowned; she seemed, Alexandra rejoiced to observe, entirely baffled.

"After your era," she said slowly, "there is—hiatus. I am not allowed give you details, for fear may influence your own report. But there was—catastrophe, and after was period of what you call chaos. It last for more than centry, then gradually control regained, and sosh sist built up to perfect govment we have today."

Alexandra suppressed a wry smile. Such smugness deserved slapping down.

"So," the historian continued, "are gaps in our detail knowl of late twenny and early twenny-one centries. Our incomplete knowl starts with very time when you lived. That why we so pleased have good cryo case at last from your era."

"The time in which I *first* lived."

"When you first lived, if prefer. That is period about which I am to question you. But now you say were two kinds of history, official and real. That is hard to believe, but if true then course we want the real history. Only, tell me—from your dossier merely private citizen, primitive computer programmer by job. How, then, if some of your history hidden from people at large, would you know anything about it?"

Alexandra drew a deep breath.

"Well," she said demurely, "I had another occupation—job, too. In a way, I was an undercover agent."

"A spy?"

"Not exactly. You see, I was tested and found to have strong Psi powers. So I was enlisted for—negotiations with those who were *really* running things." (Well, she *had* had some ESP, though hardly as strong as all that.) "That led to my being made eligible for freezing after it was discovered I had inoperable cancer. I would be the first of us agents to die, and I was given a message to deliver to the future."

Dr. Mayhew sniffed.

"Psi! I know what you mean by it, but pure nonsense. You might as well say you were a witch."

"The authorities in my time didn't think so. I've lost my power now—they told me the freezing might kill it." (Best say that, true or not, to avoid demands for demonstration.) "But I *was* able to communicate with our real rulers."

"Who were?"

By sheer will power Alexandra kept her face immobile and her voice unshaken.

"Extraterrestrials."

Dr. Mayhew glared at her.

"Oh, come now—what is this? A trick? You are wasting my time, young woman. Any more of this, and I report you useless to us and pass you on to physical examiners. After them—euthanase."

"Extraterrestrials," Alexandra repeated staunchly, her heart beating fast. "Have you ever heard of UFOs?"

"Delusions—your own officials investigated and exposed."

"Publicly. In actuality they knew they existed, and that they were unmanned automata sent out by manned mother ships from outer space. They discovered—all this was kept top secret—that the—you couldn't call them visitors, for they never landed, but they were observers—could not communicate by speech or sound.

"So it occurred to somebody that we might try communicating by telepathy. They searched for people with telepathic power, and I was only one of many they recruited. I was under oath not to reveal anything I learned, and I'm still not sure—"

"Don't be nutty. Don't forget you are absolutely in *our* power."

"That's just it, Dr. Mayhew. What I learned affects your time more than ours. I was given a message to deliver—but under conditions.

"They—our observers—realized that what you call the catastrophe—I can imagine its nature—was inevitable. They had hoped to reach us in time to reeducate us, but they decided it was too late. So all they could do was to get away from it themselves and send a messenger into the future, in the only way possible, to make sure it would never happen again.

"I am that messenger. As I told you, they chose me because I would be the first Psi agent to die. But I cannot deliver my message if I am to be a mere laboratory specimen who will be killed at the end of my usefulness. I must have a right to live my second life as a full citizen of your society. To make sure of that, they blocked my memory until that condition is fulfilled."

Dr. Mayhew laughed, but her laughter was slightly shrill.

"Very clever, Burton. Congrats; it was good effort. But nearly all cryo specimens we cured and revived were brainstruck. And those not, said no word of messages to us. Soon we explore Galaxy—then we get any messages ourselves."

Keep cool, Alexandra admonished herself.

"I didn't say," she answered calmly, "that all of us were messengers. I said *I* was. You said yourself that I am from farther back than anyone else you have resurrected. It is quite possible that the aliens sabotaged all the other cryolosis subjects in my time, to be sure that I alone should survive. And perhaps they knew they couldn't wait until you had extrasolar travel. For my message is a warning of greater catastrophes still—and I can't deliver it except as your fellow-citizen."

There was a long silence. Then the historian said, "Frank fact, doan believe you. Doan believe Psi factor exists. But I am only staff member HIP. I postpone quiries. You be called again before full meeting of Board. Meanwhile we keep you here as our guest."

As your prisoner, Alexandra reflected. Nevertheless, things were moving. Now if she could hold fast—

It gave her time, anyway—time to build up her story and do her utmost to put it over.

For it *was* a story, of course.

She knew nothing about UFOs except what she had read in the newspapers. Anybody could be frozen for cryolosis who had the money to pay for it. There had never been any "agents." She had no message from anybody to anybody. She just wanted to keep on living, and as a free individual in the world where she had awakened.

Everything, she realized, must depend on whether this highly rationalized society yet possessed some human weaknesses—whether its members were capable of curiosity, credulity, fear, even superstition. If they weren't, she was sunk. If they were, she must still produce something that would force a bargain with them.

The Board members were the same as before, with Venable as their chairman, except for one new face and one missing, that of the woman who had protested in her behalf.

By this time Alexandra was accustomed to the universal nudity, including her own. What she did still find frustrating was the fact that everybody—at least all adults, since she had seen no children—seemed to wear contact lenses, so that it was impossible to figure out their expressions. All the lenses were a frosty blue, though the usual skin color argued that by now there were few racial differences on earth.

So if Venable's glance was supposed to intimidate her, it had no effect—but neither could she read any sympathy or acceptance in his gaze.

"Have record from Mayhew your talk to-er," he began pontifically. "Explain."

"I told her," said Alexandra sturdily, "that I had Psi powers during my former life, that I had been used by the government to communicate with—"

"Know all that," the chairman interrupted her impatiently. "No need repeat. She told you was nonsense—hold to it and we destroy you as brainsick soon as through examining. This your last chance explain. Retract?"

"I hold to my story."

His voice softened.

"Burton, we are not brutes. We can unnerstan efforts to postpone, maybe escape. Confess you made up story and we forget you told it. Nicer be euthanased than—destroyed."

It was like a police interview in her own time, Alexandra thought sourly—alternately bully and wheedle, but get the confession. She had nothing to lose, so she must keep on fighting.

"What's the difference?" she asked boldly. "Whether it was true or not, I am to be killed. So there is no point in my lying to you. My story is true."

It was the last throw. If she could convince them—

"Admire your courage, Burton. Good try," said Venable dryly. "Take her back to HIP," he ordered an attendant.

So she had fought and lost, and that was that.

Or was it?

Alexandra had just a month in which to face her coming second death. She was in the middle of her examination by GAP—Genetics Assessment Program—when the aliens, finally despairing of getting their warning across to the obdurate Terrans, at last invaded Earth and wiped out the humans infesting it before they re-seeded it with a more promising race.

The last thing she had time to realize was that her lie was not a lie: that she had had far stronger Psi powers than she had guessed, and that her whole unsuccessful defense had been implanted in her mind, as a last hope, by the Extraterrestrials who had been observing mankind since the 20th century.

THE OLD BUNCH AND DUSTY STIGGINS

When Dusty Stiggins collapsed on the floor of Lou's Bar and was pronounced DOA at the Emergency Hospital, all of the Old Bunch had been there, of course. They always were. All except Dusty himself; he used to disappear for a while, but he always came back again.

So far as they could find out, he had no living relatives. Oscar Hake went around to the room he had rented for six years past, and the landlady let him in, and he searched thoroughly, but there wasn't a scrap of paper that gave any clue. She didn't know anything, either, except that he was quiet and that he always paid the rent on time, even for the periods when he was away somewhere.

So of course it was up to them. The Old Bunch always stuck together. They passed the hat around, even among other bar patrons who maybe knew Dusty only by sight or not at all, and they collected enough; Lou himself, as was to be expected, gave the most. The rest of them were all retired. Gus Durrendoerfer and Ben Wimbley had pensions, and had saved enough for their own funerals; Oscar Hake had a life insurance policy; and Chris McCaskey had a son who would see to it. They never discussed the subject, but none of them had to worry. Dusty was one of the Old Bunch, and that was that.

They did it all properly, if economically. There was an organist, and there was a wreath, and there was a preacher, suggested by the mortician (to whom he probably paid a commission). They couldn't manage much of a cemetery lot, or perpetual care, but Dusty would be long gone before the lease ran out, and once in a while on a Sunday one of them would go out there and do some weeding and maybe leave a bunch of flowers on the grave.

After two or three months they stopped talking about him, or thinking about him very often. They were used to missing him for a month or two once or twice a year, and there wasn't so much to say. Ben Wimbley remembered best how he had wandered in one rainy afternoon and they had got to talking, and he kept coming in and gradually he became one of the Bunch. "Henry Stiggins is the name," he told them, but they got to calling him Dusty because that's the way he always looked. He never said where he came from, or anything else about his past, just nursed his beer and talked about this, that, and the other thing the way they all did. If anyone in the Bunch wanted to volunteer information about himself, OK, they'd listen, but nobody ever asked questions.

So it was a terrible shock when, on another rainy afternoon about five months after the funeral, with nobody in the bar but Lou and the Old Bunch, the door opened and in walked Dusty Stiggins.

Ben Wimbley let out a screech. Chris McCaskey crossed himself. Oscar Hake, whose heart wasn't too good, had to stagger to one of the tables and fall into a chair. Only big Gus Durrendoerfer was able to use his voice. Lou just stood and stared.

"What the—you're dead!" Gus told him. Dusty just smiled.

He wasn't a ghost. He was solid. He wore the suit they'd buried him in. Lou's stare fixed on a mirror on the back wall, opposite the one behind the bar. But they could all see him in the bar mirror, and he showed in it just as they did.

He looked kind of grey and powdery, but then he always did have that kind of look. He put out his hand and grabbed Gus's, and it was a real flesh-and-bone hand.

"Thanks for the rest, boys," he said. "It was a good one. How much did it set you back?"

Oscar Hake, who'd handled the fund, said in a voice like an automatic machine, "Four hundred and thirty-two dollars." He was leaning back in the chair and breathing hard.

"And seventy-six cents," added Gus, who had been a bookkeeper before he retired.

"$432.76. I'll pay you back as soon as I can get hold of it. Who'll I give it to?"

"Oscar," said Gus. His voice was hoarse. Dusty nodded.

"A beer, Dusty?" Lou croaked. His eyes were still fixed on the back mirror.

"Not right now, Lou. I'll be seeing you." He moved in a funny sidewise motion to the door, opened it, and went out. Nobody spoke.

Lou pulled himself together. "Drink up," he said. "This round's on the house."

"Make mine whiskey, Lou," Oscar gasped. Gus carried it over to him at the table.

"You're the one always shooting off your mouth about how there's no soul and no immortality," Chris McCaskey burst out suddenly. "How about it, Gus?"

Gus cleared his throat. "You know what I think?" he said. "I think that wasn't Dusty at all. I think he's got a twin brother somewheres—an identical twin—who just found out Dusty was dead and thought it would be funny to come in here and make fools of us.

"Maybe he *will* pay the money back," he added hopefully.

"How would he know this is where Dusty hung out?" Oscar wanted to know. "How would he know our names?" But his color was coming back, and there was a distinct lift in the atmosphere.

Lou spoiled that.

"I was the only one facing him," he said. "The only one who could see him in that mirror over there.

"The back of his coat was split all the way down."

Oh, they did what they could. Oscar interviewed the landlady again—of course not telling her what had happened, just asking if anyone had inquired since about Dusty. She said no, his clothes and things were in a carton in her garage, and the room was rented. Ben Wimbley went to the cemetery and took a look at the grave. It was just the way they'd left it, except that the flowers were faded, and he threw them out. The money hadn't run to a headstone; there was just a wooden tag with a number. They'd been talking about ponying up for a plain stone. But not now.

For a while they started nervously every time the bar door opened. Oscar Hake even stayed away for two days, something that never had been known before. Chris McCaskey went around to his room in a cheap hotel, and he said he'd been to the General Hospital for a check-up on his heart. But he came back again, and nursed his beer all afternoon just like the rest of them. They never did come in after dinner; there were too many strangers then, and none of them was up to late hours any more.

So Lou was the only one who knew him who was there when Dusty Stiggins came in again.

It was almost closing time and he was busy serving last drinks. The bar was pretty crowded; it was a Friday night with a weekend ahead. He hardly noticed at first when a man pushed his way in between two stools and leaned forward, almost touching him. For a second he thought it was an obstreperous drunk who would have to be disposed of, for another second, that he was going to be held up. Then he saw who it was.

Dusty had different clothes on this time. The way funny things run through your head in a crisis, Lou wondered if he'd had to buy new ones or if he'd got his stuff somehow from the landlady's garage. He looked better than the other time, but he still looked dusty.

"Here," he said in a low voice, "give this to Oscar. I might not be around again."

He thrust a little cloth bag into Lou's hand, smiled, raised his right hand in a salute, and walked out.

Fortunately the place was emptying fast, and Lou managed to hold on until he'd got the last one out and locked the door. Then he took a double shot, straight, and let himself down on a stool. He was shaking all over.

He opened the bag and there it was—$432.76 in currency and coin, and a scrap of paper on which was written, "Give this to the boys and tell them thanks again."

"But, good Lord," Ben Wimbley said the next day when Lou told them about it, "grant he could have got out of there—but how?—and grant he could fix the grave up again. But you know and I know, they embalm people before they bury them. I had a cousin once started to be an undertaker—he got the whoops about it and never finished the training—but he told me how they drain out the fluids and whatever and inject embalming fluid instead. And embalming fluid has a lot of formaldehyde in it, and that's poison."

"Yeah," Gus Durrendoerfer added, "and besides all that, where would old Dusty ever get that much money? He never seemed to have more than enough to live on, all these years."

"Do you think," Chris McCaskey asked hesitantly, "maybe it's just somebody *impersonating* him?"

"Rats," Oscar Hake objected. "That sounds like one of them Gothic novels, they call them. Why *should* anybody, for heaven's sake—$432 worth?"

"And 76 cents," Lou chimed in. "And what's more, it *was* Dusty, both times. Nobody could fake that queer voice of his."

That was one reason he'd got the nickname; even his voice sounded as if he were breathing dust.

Gus shook his bald head. "It's like a bad dream," he said. "It couldn't happen, and yet it did. I wonder where he is now?"

"Wherever he is, and whatever he is, I have a hunch we won't see him here again," said Lou. "Drink up, boys; it's on me again."

Around three o'clock that morning, the thing that called itself Henry Stiggins had got back to the cemetery. He made the neat accustomed incision and climbed in wearily. It was an accident he regretted, having the collapse come upon him suddenly like that, in public; usually he knew in advance and could be near his current grave. Embalming fluid would substitute for blood for just so long, and perhaps with the years his resistance was growing weaker.

Still, this was a nice grave and it had been good of the Old Bunch to give him such a fine send-off. He knew very well they couldn't really afford it; that's why he'd made up his mind to repay them. It had taken five muggings and a murder to raise enough for that. But now it was done and he could have a good long rest again before he made tracks for another town, under another name.

Even a ghoul has his moments of friendliness and gratitude.